Samuel French Acting Edition

I0591738

The Earth is Flat

by Todd Almond

SAMUELFRENCH.COM   SAMUELFRENCH.CO.UK

FOR PRODUCTION ENQUIRIES

UNITED STATES AND CANADA
Info@SamuelFrench.com
1-866-598-8449

UNITED KINGDOM AND EUROPE
Plays@SamuelFrench.co.uk
020-7255-4302

Each title is subject to availability from Samuel French, depending
upon country of performance. Please be aware that *THE EARTH
IS FLAT* may not be licensed by Samuel French in your territory.
Professional and amateur producers should contact the nearest Samuel
French office or licensing partner to verify availability.

MUSIC USE NOTE

Licensees are solely responsible for obtaining formal written permission from copyright owners to use copyrighted music in the performance of this play and are strongly cautioned to do so. If no such permission is obtained by the licensee, then the licensee must use only original music that the licensee owns and controls. Licensees are solely responsible and liable for all music clearances and shall indemnify the copyright owners of the play(s) and their licensing agent, Samuel French, against any costs, expenses, losses and liabilities arising from the use of music by licensees. Please contact the appropriate music licensing authority in your territory for the rights to any incidental music.

IMPORTANT BILLING AND CREDIT REQUIREMENTS

If you have obtained performance rights to this title, please refer to your licensing agreement for important billing and credit requirements.

THE EARTH IS FLAT was commissioned as part of the CCM Playwrights Workshop and premiered in the Cohen Family Studio Theatre at the University of Cincinnati College-Conservatory of Music on November 2, 2017. The production was directed by Richard E. Hess, with scenic design by Levi Kiess, lighting design by Elanor Eberhardt, costume design by Ashley Trujillo, and sound design by Josh Windes. The production stage manager was Caroline Castleman. The cast was as follows:

ETHAN	Jack Steiner
DEREK	Graham Lutes
JENNIFER	Olivia Passafiume & Madeleine Page-Schmit
SHELLEY	Carissa Cardy & Meg Olson
GUY WHO LOOKS LIKE JEREMY	Carter LaCava
MEN VARIOUS	Graham Rogers
WOMEN VARIOUS	Paige Jordan

CHARACTERS

ETHAN
DEREK
JENNIFER
SHELLEY
GUY WHO LOOKS LIKE JEREMY
MEN VARIOUS
WOMEN VARIOUS

AUTHOR'S NOTES

The Earth is Flat is about the forging of a (best) friendship. It's difficult to truly know the importance of a relationship while it is forming, but what we watch when we watch Ethan and Derek struggle and succeed and struggle and succeed some more, is that very (best) friend formation. I wanted to pay tribute to that with the play. My best friend (whom I met in college) saved my life by giving me the Heimlich maneuver. How can I ever repay him?

Of course Ethan's quest for identity is the driving force of the play, and I just love the thought of him being GIVEN identities by others, which manifest mostly in his hair color and style.

Some thoughts that might help:

1. I don't judge any of these characters. All of them, not just Ethan, are trying to figure out just who the hell they are. There's no enemy in this play.

2. There are no gender or race requirements. I suspect the play resonates in different ways based on the casting choices, so I encourage you to feel free to explore these characters' identities yourself.

3. There are many characters who appear for a line or two to "people" the world. (This serves the function of bringing Derek and Ethan closer together because they get the shared experience of witnessing these personalities over the course of their short two days together in the dorm before Ethan must leave.) But for your specific production it provides two distinct casting possibilities: One – a chance to cast a lot of people or Two – a chance to give two actors the challenge of playing multiple characters. In the premiere production, director Richard Hess chose option two. And the actors playing multiple roles had a great time scene-stealing. But the choice is yours.

4. My alma mater is the College-Conservatory of Music at the University of Cincinnati (or CCM, for less of a mouthful), and I love that school. *The*

Earth is Flat is full of references to the school (dorms), the surrounding area (street names), and inside jokes (a rival school). I think you should, should you desire to, replace these references with references to your own school or area. Of course, you don't HAVE to, but I'm a sucker for laughs, and inside jokes tend to wring them just the way I like.

ACT ONE

Scene One
Arrival

(A dormitory hallway of a large midwestern state university. It's been abused over the years.)

(Several closed, numbered doors, most with dry-erase boards attached. Various stupid things written on them.)

(One open door with cheap public seating in view. The lounge.)

(From one closed door we hear a sudden loud eruption of despair from a group of boys. Like a beloved football team just fumbled [which is in fact what happened]. One of the boys coughs a lot. Someone laughs at him.)

(We see an average young man but with purple hair, ETHAN, enter the hallway. He's got a backpack on and a welcome packet in one hand. The packet says "802" in large numbers. He looks for room 802. It is at the end of the hallway.)

(The dry-erase board outside of 802 says: "E is F." ETHAN reads it.)

(ETHAN pulls a key from the packet and unlocks room 802.)

(When he opens the door, we again hear a very loud shout of despair from the group – only this time we see them, briefly, because the group is inside room 802. The sight

> startles **ETHAN** *and he quickly slams the door closed.)*
>
> *(He makes a startled noise.)*
>
> *(He stands in the hallway. Checks the packet: 802. Checks the door: 802. This is the right room.)*
>
> *(He looks at his watch, it's late.)*
>
> *(He's tired.)*
>
> *(He opens the door to room 802 again, slowly. Peeks in. The guys inside cheer at the TV.)*
>
> *(***ETHAN*** closes the door, leans against the wall, headfirst.)*

ETHAN. *(Sighing.) Fuuuuuck.*

> *(He slumps to the floor. Closes his eyes for a minute. He's clearly exhausted.)*
>
> *(A door marked "Men" opens, and a handsome young man, ***DEREK***, walks out.)*
>
> *(He steps over ***ETHAN*** on the floor. ***ETHAN*** is startled.)*

DEREK. Oh, sorry, sorry.

> *(***ETHAN*** grumpily moans.)*

You...?

> *(Louder, grumpier moan from ***ETHAN***.)*

Okay.

> *(Someone exits one of the other rooms and slams their door hard. Bang!)*

ETHAN. *(Still slumped and grumpy.)* Why is everyone so loud? Today? Why is it so hard to be...like...*quiet*? Not everyone wants to hear your door slam or your stupid conversation on the airplane. Or... *(Grumpy moan.)*

DEREK. All right, man. Well...

(Shouts with college pride.) U.C.!

> *(***ETHAN*** is annoyed at how loud that was.)*

(**DEREK**, *over this whole interaction, opens the door to room 802.*)

ETHAN. You know. That's *my* room.

DEREK. That's *my* room.

(*Realizing this is his roommate.*)

Oh.

(*Disappointed.*) Really?

ETHAN. Yeah.

(*Silence.*)

DEREK. Derek.

ETHAN. Ethan.

DEREK. I was expecting you a lot earlier, thought maybe something had...

ETHAN. No, just... (*Groan/sigh.*)

(*The door for 802 flies open, and a young man, **MARK**, flies out of the room down the hallway toward the bathroom.*)

MARK. I've had to piss for like an hour! Ha! Purple Hair! Holy shit, man.

(**MARK** *disappears behind the door marked "Men."*)

ETHAN. Awesome.

(*Re: the guys in his room.*) What's with...?

DEREK. Oh.

(**DEREK** *opens the door and the guys inside are crowding the room so completely that there's really no room for **ETHAN**. The guys don't react to the door opening. They are completely engrossed in a football game. And beers. And whatever.*)

Hey, guys...?

(*This time the guys cheer at something that happened on the screen. They make a lot of noise and drown out **DEREK** as he tries to speak.*)

ETHAN. *(Shouting.)* It's okay! I can wait outside!

DEREK. *(Shouting.)* What?!

> (**DEREK** *steps back out, closes the door.*)

Jeez. Loud.

ETHAN. Yeah. I know.

DEREK. Sorry –

> (*Silence. This is not going well.* **MARK** *runs back through, to 802.*)

MARK. Dude, you're out of vodka –

> (*Suddenly,* **MARK** *drunkenly stumbles.*)

> (**ETHAN** *miraculously catches him and stabilizes him.*)

Purple Hair! Freaky.

> (**MARK** *is gone.*)

DEREK. Nice one.

ETHAN. What, catching a stumbling drunk? Lotta practice.

DEREK. I know, man. High school was awesome.

ETHAN. That's not what I... I'll just go get something to eat, I haven't...all day...and I saw like three places across the street, so, it's cool, I'm cool, you can have...a party or...

DEREK. Just watching the game...

ETHAN. ....Just at some point I'll...

DEREK. ...Not a *party*.

ETHAN. ...Need to get in there.

> (*Looks around at how empty-handed he is.*)

When my stuff...

DEREK. Oh, yeah. Where is your stuff? Don't you have stuff?

ETHAN. My stuff. My stuff is...I don't know where. *Vanished.* All of my stuff, so...like, *everything*. I guess. Who knows?

DEREK. Vanished?

ETHAN. Vanished.

DEREK. Weird.

ETHAN. *Vanished.*

DEREK. How?

ETHAN. Well...

> *(Reluctantly tells his story.)*

...I missed my first flight, my mom got lost on the way to the airport – I don't know why I let her drive, she was suddenly so *motherly*, and so I caved. *The first of my children, the first of my* family *to go to college, I* want *to drive you.* So I actually let her...and then she missed the exit because she was crying, *Who's going to keep your sister in line now? Who's going to take care of my*...anyway, so I caught a later flight. But then when I landed, my *stuff*, if you can *believe* it – Whatever. Who cares?

(New thought.) You know how you're *not* supposed to say *I'm starving* because there are people who are actually starving? *I'm starving.*

> *(**DEREK** suddenly walks away and goes into the room, closing the door behind him. Leaving **ETHAN** alone in the hallway.)*

Oh. Bye.

> *(**DEREK** re-emerges with a bag of chips and a beer. He hands the chips to **ETHAN**, drinks the beer himself.)*

DEREK. Here.

ETHAN. *(Surprised.)* Oh. Thank you.

> *(His bad day is suddenly improving.)*

Chips.

> *(Eating.)*

Perfect.

> *(While **ETHAN** eats chips, a young man, **JAMES**, steps out of room 804 and sits on the floor, just outside the door, on his phone. He clearly does not want his roommate to hear his conversation.)*

JAMES. Well, Dad, just look at the email I sent you. It says right... I'll just read it to you. These are all of our breaks for the year, so I want to... I can come home for all of them, so just book the tickets now so that I have them. There's fall break, Veterans Day in November, I can come home for twenty-four hours. Thanksgiving, Christmas through New Year's, but you booked that, tell me you booked that already, right? Should I just stay from Thanksgiving on? I don't know why I'd *need* to come back to school for only two weeks before Christmas. I'll just stay from Thanksgiving through New Year's. Then Martin Luther King Junior Day, I'll come for the long weekend. Spring break. The *whole* thing. And then my birthday week. Email me confirmation. Tonight, okay?

> (**JAMES** *finally notices that* **DEREK** *and* **ETHAN** *are also in the hallway. He is embarrassed.*)

Oh.

> (**JAMES** *goes into his dorm room.*)

> (**ETHAN** *and* **DEREK** *smile at each other.*)

ETHAN. So I guess that means he'll be spending Arbor Day alone?

> (**DEREK** *laughs.*)

DEREK. Gotta get some me-time somewhere.

> (**ETHAN** *laughs.*)

ETHAN. I wonder if the dorms stay open during the holidays? Do we, like, *have* to go home?

> (*Suspicious of* **DEREK**'s *beer.*)

Surely that can't be...like, *allowed*, right?

DEREK. Oh, it's not. But everyone's already... I don't think they really care. The RA is in my room. Our room.

ETHAN. Huh. People used to drink in high school.

DEREK. Not you?

> (**ETHAN** *wolfs down chips. Sighs.*)

ETHAN. I feel better already. Sorry I was such a grump. Probably not how you imagined meeting your roommate.

DEREK. Well it *was* a little...the hair, the grunting.

(**ETHAN** *laughs.*)

Like this little emo zombie.

ETHAN. Oh, god! Is that what you...?

DEREK. Well. (*Points at his hair.*) I'd grunt, too, honestly, if I showed up to school and a bunch of...*bros* were in my space.

ETHAN. *Bros.* No, it's cool. It's nice, actually – I was hoping to...let loose a little in college. I should be thanking you – we're the popular room already. *U.C.!*

(**ETHAN** *steals* **DEREK***'s beer and takes a swig to show he's letting loose. Makes a face – it's terrible.*)

(*Spits some out.*)

(*Yuck.*)

(*Beat.*)

DEREK. You didn't finish.

ETHAN. It's not really for me.

DEREK. No, your story. How did your stuff...*vanish*?

ETHAN. Oh. God. Okay. I flew from Denver with these enormous, very *heavy*, these...huge boxes. We've never had suitcases for some reason...never needed them, I guess... My mom was so concerned: *How are you going to get these damn boxes from the airport to the dorm? No taxi is going to pick you up with your purple hair.* And I said: *Then FedEx them to me, or drive me to college* – Ha! Ha! – *if you're so worried. And then no one will be subjected to my purple hair.* She said: *It's so expensive, and I don't know why you have to go so far away to school. And I can't take two days off of work to drive you to college.* And I said: *I'll figure it out! Whatever.* And then people at the airport said...

DEREK. (*Interrupting.*) There's a lounge right there. Couches.

ETHAN. Oh. Sure.

(Re: chips.) These are saving my life. Thank you.

DEREK. Yep.

ETHAN. *Derek*, right?

DEREK. Yup. Jeremy, was it?

ETHAN. Ethan.

DEREK. Where'd I get *Jeremy*?

> *(They walk into the lounge. After a second they quickly exit, holding their noses and scampering back to just outside room 802.)*

Oh, man...!

ETHAN. If that came out of a human body, that person should seek immediate medical attention.

> *(**DEREK** laughs.)*

I may burn these shoes.

DEREK. Ha. Man. That's disgusting.

ETHAN. Could we just sit *here*? It's so comfy and nice and these chips are so freaking delicious, what kind of *chips* are these? I'm a new man. I swear.

DEREK. Good. So, your mom was being a monster and didn't want to drive you to college. And?

ETHAN. Did I say that?

DEREK. Yeah – you had giant boxes, she refused to ship them, she wouldn't take time off of work to drive her son to college, but that's probably good because she's a reckless driver, she let you fly alone with all of your heavy stuff, she bitched about your hair...

ETHAN. That's what came across to you, about my mom, from what I said? That she's a horrible person?

DEREK. Not horrible. Not nice, but.

ETHAN. Hmm.

> *(Gets lost in the thought of what he thinks about his mother.)*

DEREK. So *what happened to the boxes*?!

ETHAN. Oh, right...

> *(Can't let it go.)*

She really *can't* take days off of work to drive me here, she barely makes enough to pay the rent, and now this loan for me to be here, well, I'll be paying back the loan... It's not like she's a bad mom or like a drunk or something. Well, she's kind of a drunk. More like, pills...but not a pill addict, more like...she can't stop taking prescription she's a pill addict. Fuck. Yeah. It's a problem. My mom is a raging pill addict and –

> *(Suddenly **ETHAN** jumps up and does a little dance and makes up an impromptu song.)*

I'M NEVER GOING BACK, I'M NEVER GOING BACK, DENVER COLORADO CAN EAT MY BLANK BECAUSE I'M NEVER GOING BACK! God! It was actually like a horror movie, getting out of there...

> *(A young **WOMAN**, looking very lost, walks through...)*

LOST GIRL. Are you Brian?

DEREK. No.

ETHAN. No.

LOST GIRL. Do you know Brian?

DEREK. No.

ETHAN. No.

LOST GIRL. What floor is this?

DEREK & ETHAN. Eight.

LOST GIRL. And you're not Brian?

ETHAN. *(No.)* Hmm-mmm.

> *(The **LOST GIRL** goes looking for Brian.)*

(Picking right back up.) ...Like a HORROR movie getting out of there, you know, where the lead character is *this close* to escaping, but then...oh, no, the car breaks down! Oh, no, the monster is just about to grab you and pull you back. Oh, no! You missed the flight...

the monster is snatching at you, closer, closer, ahh!...
But then...

(*Slams down to the ground.*)

Shhhwoooooshhhh. He's makes it out. And the very
last scene is him sitting on the hallway floor outside
of his dorm room, with his new roommate Derek, and
they're eating the best chips anyone has ever eaten in
the world. Credits.

(**DEREK** *sings a little impromptu credits music.**)

Nice.

(*Beat.*)

She was so upset that I dyed my hair purple...

DEREK. Catholic?

ETHAN. Lutheran. Why?

DEREK. You seem Catholic. (*Raised hand.*) Catholic. Mass
on Sunday, every Sunday, Catholic middle school, public
high school, CCD on Wednesday. My *very* reverent,
very nosy, very never-popped-a-pill-in-this-or-any-
other-lifetime parents drove me all the way here from
Chicago. They actually stayed here – waiting in the
lounge! Gross! – For hours just to meet you. Wanted
to make sure my roommate wasn't some heroin junkie
or Satan worshiper. They gave up, eventually – now I'll
have to tell them you're a purple-haired Protestant with
a pill-popping, negligent mother.

ETHAN. No!

(*Laughs.*)

She's not...she makes Christmas tree cookies year-
round! She pops pills, she thinks it's Christmas every
day!

(*Laughs hard at this.*)

---

*A license to produce *The Earth is Flat* does not include a performance
license for any third-party or copyrighted music. Licensees should create
an original composition or use music in the public domain. For further
information, please see Music Use Note on page 3.

Oh, god, why is that so funny to me? It's not funny! But it's hilarious. Right? God, I hope she made it home from the airport. Or. I don't care.

(Touches his hair; he doesn't like it.)

My. Hair. Is. Purple.

DEREK. I like it. You're so cool. I love it. It's awesome. I love it.

ETHAN. You *do*? My sister dyed it. She convinced me – she told me to loosen up, that I needed to step up my game, moving to the big city.

DEREK. This is *Cincinnati.*

ETHAN. I know.

DEREK. Who are you trying to impress?

ETHAN. No one. Everyone. I don't know.

> *(The **LOST GIRL** returns, still very confused and lost.)*

LOST GIRL. Do you know what time it is?

DEREK. Uhh...ten oh six, p.m.

LOST GIRL. *Dang it.*

> *(**LOST GIRL** goes.)*

DEREK. I could never dye my hair bright purple.

ETHAN. Well, my sister said...college feels like a good chance to become who I really am, and that, uh, how did she say it...that, uh... She had *all sorts* of great reasons why I should dye my hair purple, if only she were here, she could explain them to you.

DEREK. You're funny.

ETHAN. If Jennifer told you to dye your hair purple, you would.

DEREK. Nope. Not that cool. *Finish your story – what happened to the boxes, how did they vanish?!*
Oh, but, by the way: what a relief that you're easy to talk to. I thought for sure I'd get some moron who was dead-serious and drooled. This is great.

ETHAN. Yeah. Me, too. Me, too.

DEREK. The boxes.

ETHAN. Oh my god! It is the most boring story ever told, I can't believe it's still coming out of my mouth. So the airline lost my stuff, you know, just like how they lose luggage sometimes?

DEREK. Oh.

ETHAN. Yeah.

DEREK. That's it?

ETHAN. That's it. Fascinating, right?

DEREK. You made it sound like it was going to be more… you said *vanished*…so I was imagining…

ETHAN. I know, I'm a horrible person. I'm sorry I led you on like that. And to add insult to injury, the story's not actually over: The people at the airport said Not To Worry, We Will Deliver Your Things To Your House. I said: My *Dorm*! They said: Nothing, they just walked away. Rude. So if there is anything redeeming about this soul-sucking tale it is that I am in fact *relieved* that they lost my luggage, because I truly didn't know how I was going to get those huge boxes here, but now it's THEIR problem. That's the whole story.

DEREK. The End.

ETHAN. Aren't you glad you kept insisting that I finish?

DEREK. I liked the crazy mom part.

ETHAN. *(Smiles.)* This is cool. I was worried, too. About who you would be. This is just what I needed. I LOVE COLLEGE.

> *(A quiet and slightly mysterious young* **MAN** *walks down the hall and past* **ETHAN** *and* **DEREK**. *For some reason it's strange.)*

Did you see that?

DEREK. That guy?

ETHAN. Yeah – wow, he looked *exactly* like my brother.

DEREK. Really? Huh.

ETHAN. *Exactly.* I thought it was *him* for a second. But my brain froze up – what would Jeremy be doing here? Isn't that strange?

DEREK. Yeah. Wow. Oh, *that's* where I got "Jeremy." You said your brother's name.

ETHAN. I did?

> *(Another boy appears. **STEVE**.)*
>
> *(He is walking and looking at his phone, not looking where he's going.)*
>
> *(He trips over **DEREK**.)*

STEVE. Sorry.

> *(Still not looking up, he trips over **ETHAN**.)*

Sorry.

> *(**STEVE** goes into the lounge, lays on the couch, reads.)*

ETHAN. Umm – hey, you know there's...uh...

DEREK. There's a wet pile of freshman hoark right by the couch there.

STEVE. Huh? Oh. Yeah. That's nasty.

> *(**STEVE** stays on the couch and keeps looking at his phone.)*

DEREK. *(Horrified.)* Nice.

> *(**DEREK** and **ETHAN** laugh together, quietly, so **STEVE** doesn't hear them laughing.)*

Should we talk about – roommate stuff, just get it out of the way, like rules and things, or just let it naturally evolve?

ETHAN. We should probably talk about it. I guess. You seem like you'll be easy.

DEREK. Same. Okay. Umm. So, like, no stinky food, right? Things covered in ketchup? Smells so bad – and we sleep in there, so. Smell. I think smell is probably the number one. I mean, I have foot spray and mouthwash and matches even, that you can use, you know, and even, uh, a box of candles that I brought. For this problem.

ETHAN. Do I smell bad?

DEREK. No. I don't think so.

> (**DEREK** *smells* **ETHAN**.)

> (*It's suddenly a touch awkward for* **ETHAN**.)

No. You smell fine.

ETHAN. Really? I've been on a plane all day. I feel…

DEREK. You actually smell kinda good.

> (**ETHAN** *is embarrassed.*)

> (**JAMES** *re-emerges from his room. He kind of hovers awkwardly near the boys like he wants to say something, or engage with them in some way, but he doesn't know how.*)

DEREK. I hate bad smells. Pizza? Disgusting smell, after. Ugh. For days. So no pizza. Or ketchup. Or just, how about *no food.*

ETHAN. Okay. Fine.

JAMES. *(Weirdly.)* Pizza.

DEREK. Umm…oh, don't hit on my girlfriend. Obviously. When I have one. Which I will.

> (**DEREK** *crosses his fingers.*)

ETHAN. Okay. Not a problem. *At all.*

DEREK. You got a…? *Oh, wait,* are you…?

ETHAN. Yeah, I'm.

DEREK. Oh, okay. That's cool.

ETHAN. You've got a cousin, right?

DEREK. What?

ETHAN. That's what people always say: Oh, you're gay? That's cool. I've got a cousin…

JAMES. *(Laughs.)* So true.

DEREK. Well, I *do* have a cousin, actually. *Lesbian*. But I wasn't going to say that. In fact, I have like *five* cousins.

ETHAN. Not me. Well, *one*. He annoys me. He's like, *that* kinda gay guy. You know?

DEREK. No.

ETHAN. Oh.

LOST GIRL. *(From offstage.)* BRIIIIAAAAANNNNN!

JAMES. Are you Brian? 'Cause someone is looking for you.

ETHAN. Ethan.

DEREK. Derek.

(To **ETHAN**.*)* You can have guys over if you want. When I'm not here. And I can have – when you're not.

ETHAN. Okay.

DEREK. What else?

JAMES. Food and sex, those are the basics.

(They both look at **JAMES**.*)*

DEREK. Drugs?

ETHAN. No.

DEREK. Me, neither. Beer. Liquor. Definitely. Oh, man, so rude. You didn't like the beer, but I think you'll love the...you wanna try something else?

ETHAN. Umm...sure. Okay.

JAMES. I'm allergic.

DEREK. Hold on.

*(***DEREK** *goes into 802, brings back some horrible liquor.)*

It's cheap, sorry – quickest I could find. I'll get better stuff...

JAMES. Who are those guys?

DEREK. Oh. I don't know. Jeremy, I think?

ETHAN. That's my brother's name.

DEREK. Brandon something. And Daryl.

ETHAN. You don't know them?

DEREK. I don't know anyone here – you! I know you!

JAMES. James.

DEREK. I met these guys at the, in the, I think they all live on this floor. I don't know. I put the game on TV and – they just kinda showed up. It's just...it's how guys are. *That* kinda straight guy. You know?

JAMES. So true.

ETHAN. I'm starting to crash.

DEREK. You know what, this is, I'm being such a jerk about this... I'm going to kick them out.

> *(Goes into the room.)*

Hey, guys – hey, I gotta kick you out, my roommate finally showed up...

GUY #1. Is she hot?

DEREK. So, thanks for kicking off the school year with me. You can watch the game in the lounge.

> *(The **GUYS** file from 802 to the lounge. Suddenly a dorm front-desk **EMPLOYEE** [really just a student doing work-study, male or female] appears.)*

WORK-STUDY KID. Excuse me, do you know who Ethan Jeffrey is?

DEREK. *(In the room.)* Funny.

ETHAN. That's me.

WORK-STUDY KID. You have like five enormous boxes on the elevator.

WORK-STUDY KID.	**GUY #2.**
I can't move them. You need to...	Game's not over, dude.

JAMES. Do you need any help, or?

DEREK. You can watch in the lounge.

STEVE. I'm reading in here!

WORK-STUDY KID.

Someone from the airport
just dropped them off and
was like:
These belong here. And
then they drove away.
But I'm not a bellhop.
I've been calling and
calling your room.
Since you won't answer,
you should make sure
people know to call your
cell phone so you can
come down to the lobby
to meet them, because
I almost threw my back
out putting these on
the elevator and I'm not
really supposed to do a
lot of heavy lifting after
my surgery. I don't even
want to work at the front
desk, but to get the crappy
like five-thousand dollar
scholarship that the
Kiwanis Club gave me,
I have to do work-study.
So it's like not even a
scholarship at all, it's like
a job that pays pretty low
wages and that I don't
really want to do. So it's
not worth my undoing the
very painful surgery that I
had to endure just to bring
you some boxes.

*(The door to 802 closes,
but we hear shuffling
about.)*

JAMES.

I love Kiwanis.

They have a talent show.

(The elevator beeps.)

WORK-STUDY KID.

And now the elevator is acting up because I had to prop the doors open, and you don't know this and you didn't hear it from me, but there is something *off* about that elevator. It's not fast, but it feels like it's flying. It's a little alarming. Plus it gets caught in-between floors and then you're stuck there. It happened to me twice already. So you need to get them right now or else the elevator will stop working and everyone will have to use the stairs and I'm NOT supposed to take stairs for like three more months until I am absolutely healed.

JAMES.

I won. Third.

Flute solo.

Theme song to *Friends*.

ETHAN. Okay. Okay, I'll get them.

WORK-STUDY KID. Do I sound like my mother?

ETHAN. I don't know your mother.

WORK-STUDY KID. I do! I do!

DEREK. *(Gesturing to the now-empty room 802.)* The room's all yours!

ETHAN. Cheers! What does that mean – E is F? On the board, there?

DEREK. Oh. It means...umm...

> *(He takes the attached marker and writes on the dry-erase board.)*

Ethan is Finally here.

ETHAN. Finally!

>   (**DEREK** *chugs an entire beer. Then opens another. Chugs it, too.*)

DEREK. Let's move some BOXES!!

JAMES. Yay!

>   (*Blackout.*)

Scene Two
Departure

(The next day.)

(The same hallway. **ETHAN** *is in the hallway with the same boxes.)*

(We hear the ding of the unseen elevator – **DEREK**, *who is pretty drunk, enters.)*

DEREK. More boxes?! Man, I'm starting to take your mom's side – you have *a lot* of shit. I don't think we've got any more *(Hiccup.)* room.

ETHAN. Same boxes.

DEREK. Garbage? Oh, cool. Need help? I'm a little drunk, though. I'm a little drunk. *DRUNK!* You want a beer? Do we have beer? You hate beer. Let's have a beer and then we'll take your garbage down...

ETHAN. Just packing them back up. The...boxes.

DEREK. Why?

> *(Silence.)*

Why?

> *(Silence.)*

Why are you packing your boxes?

> *(Silence.)*

Are you moving out?

> *(Silence.)*

Oh, man, you're moving out?!

> *(Silence.)*

What the...? One night and you're moving out? I thought we... Oh, man. What? What's wrong? Do my feet stink? I knew it! Shit.

ETHAN. No.

DEREK. Is it the alcohol? I know, I think I drink too much, I think maybe it's a problem. Shhh!

ETHAN. No.

DEREK. Did I say something to upset you? Why...you're moving out? I thought we kinda hit it off. I thought... *Don't move out, man, come on*, was it the party? Aww, come on, we're in college now, we're supposed to have parties. It was the first night, it's not like you had some big test to study for. Ahh, man. This is hurting my feelings. Why didn't you just say, "Derek, don't throw parties. And you stink, man. Your feet fucking stink!"

> *(Suddenly upset.)*

You know what, man, *you* need to party. You need to embrace the spir...in brace the...in brace? Embrace the...you have purple hair, dude, you're a rebel, act like it. Come on, don't...

ETHAN. It's not the party, it's not that... I'm...going home. Back home.

DEREK. You don't like it here? It's fucking DAY TWO, man. You can't give up on DAY TWO! What? Some asshole say something to you? I'll punch him out. Done. Stay. What? You don't like some class? Just drop it. Just you just you just walk over to the regstra...resistrar... and you say, "I'd like to drop Professor Asshole's class because he's a bad teacher and he touched me."

> *(Laughs.)*

Come on, Ethan, I'm moving your boxes back in. This is ridiculous, I'm not letting you quit college because of Pofressor Asswipe.

ETHAN. Derek.

DEREK. Ethan.

> *(Silence.)*

> *(Mocking, joking.) ETHAN.*

>> (**DEREK** *picks up a box and tries to move it back into 802.)*

ETHAN. Derek. Stop. I really... I have to... My... I have, like...a family thing...and...I need to go back home

and... I just, I... I've got to go to the airport and I have
to buy a ticket I guess, or... I need...can you...?

DEREK. No, no, no! You're staying here, buddy boy. Look at
the board: Ethan is Finally here. Ethan is Free! Ethan
is Fucking awesome.

  (**ETHAN** *gives a weird look.*)

Are you okay?

  (**ETHAN** *is not okay.*)

Aw, man. What? What is it? You're being all...

  (*Horrible silence.*)

Sit down, man. What's going on?

  (**ETHAN** *is full of a horrible truth.*)

Tell me, man, I'm your roommate, I'm your best friend
so far at college, and you gotta tell your best-friend
what's wrong. It's the rule.

ETHAN. Umm. It's. My brother...like, I guess...got into a
really bad motorcycle accident. Or. Back home. So.
Yeah. It's okay. He's...just...he's a really vital, athletic
guy, you know? He's...the kind of person who will climb
mountains one day, just because he can...you know?
He's... Yeah, he's...he's older than me, and, like...you
know that stupid expression "old soul." People don't say
that to me because I'm not. But he is that. He's...really
comfortable in the world, like, easy. He knows how to
move, how to live, umm...as if he's been here forever
and he loves it and it loves him back... I'm not...saying
it right...

It's all so... He was on his bike – he rides his motorcycle
everywhere which is just another thing that makes
him so...cool...my sister, she called me, said he...the
bike flipped or something, and... I don't know...driving
late at night, or...maybe another car... I couldn't quite
understand her because the world started skipping
and I couldn't, like, hear her very well...so... I don't
mean to be so dramatic right now, I think she said...
it's so stupid that I don't know exactly what she said...

but she said, I'm pretty sure...umm...she said that he died? Only, I don't see how he could die when he's, like, the most alive person I've ever known, so, maybe I misunderstood her...just...I don't...

(Silence.)

Didn't we see him last night? Remember, he walked right past us.

(Silence.)

DEREK. I'm so sorry. Fuck. I'm sorry I'm drunk. I really hate that I'm drunk right now.

*(**ETHAN** is silent.)*

Ethan. Ethan.

ETHAN. It's...like...the world is one of those flip books, where a little cartoon character dances, only the person thumbing through the pages isn't very good at it and so each page...kind of jerks by and I can't make it smooth again.

(Silence.)

DEREK. I don't know what to say.

ETHAN. It's messed up, right?

DEREK. It's messed up. Ethan, I'm...just... I don't ever want to... FUCK!...I don't ever want to drink again. Mother of...! I hate this. I don't...

(Long silence.)

*(**JAMES**, the guy who made the telephone call earlier, steps into the hallway on the phone again.)*

JAMES. No, it's something about the river and the hills, there are these hills which create like pollen vortexes and I honestly can't breathe. It's worse than asthma. I will *try* to learn to breathe with the partial lung-capacity to which I'm now reduced, but I can't promise that I will succeed. So. If we can't find a solution, I may need to look to transferring to somewhere out there, where I know I can breathe. Or I could just die. I could just die. You could just leave your son here to die of pollen asphyxiation. Well! Maybe! Goodbye.

(**JAMES** *again sees* **DEREK** *and* **ETHAN** *in the hallway.*)

Oh. You guys live in this hallway.

(**JAMES** *goes.*)

DEREK. So you're going to go to the airport? Now?

ETHAN. I guess. I'm kinda...

DEREK. Yeah. I can take you. I can take you. In a cab. I can't *drive* you.

ETHAN. 'Cause you're drunk?

DEREK. YES! Fuck!! Why?! Oh, god! How do I get not drunk right now? This is the worst feeling.

(*Slaps himself.*)

Not drunk! Not drunk!

ETHAN. You are hilarious.

DEREK. I hate it. You need me right now and I'm like standing in the deep end of a glass swimming pool looking at you on the outside. And the water is very slowly draining, but it's gonna be a while until I'm not underwater anymore. So all I can do is watch you and know that you need me, but I can't help you until the stupid slow drain let's all this booze out.

ETHAN. You *sound* sober.

DEREK. I used to get obliterated in high school and no one knew.

ETHAN. They knew.

DEREK. No! Nobody knew.

ETHAN. I bet they knew.

DEREK. (*Starts crying.*) Oh, don't say that. You're making fun of me. I'm so sorry I'm drunk. I'm so sorry that your brother died. That's the worst thing I can imagine.

ETHAN. (*Laughs a little at* **DEREK**'s *melodrama.*) You're so drunk.

DEREK. Why are you laughing?! None of this is funny. It's the most tragic thing that has ever happened in my life so far. I made a friend and now he's suffering and I'm fucking wasted and I can't even help him.

ETHAN. Okay, now you're a little pathetic. But it's helping 'cause it's effing hilarious.

DEREK. Ethan. Do you want me to go with you to Den, *(Hiccup.)* Den, *(Hiccup.)* Den, *(Hiccup.)* Colorado?

ETHAN. No. No.

> *(Laughs at the hiccups.)*

No. Nope.

DEREK. Because I would.

ETHAN. That's very nice of you.

DEREK. 'Cause I am really good at killing monsters.

ETHAN. Monsters?

DEREK. I'm sorry that my feet stink. It's always bothered me. I'm sorry that I'm this drunk. I keep saying that. I'm sorry that the world is such an asshole. I'm your best friend in this asshole world and I'm letting you down. Nooooo.

ETHAN. Oh, *(Touches* **DEREK***'s head.)* you didn't make the world.

> *(They sit on the floor.)*

DEREK. Some people think the world is flat. Did you know that? This old idea has come back again. They're crazy – conspi...spear...conpse... I can't say it,...conpearcer... ugh!

ETHAN. Conspiracy theorists?

DEREK. Conpirsiry thurtis. Yeah. The earth is flat. The government is lying to us. They know it's flat, and they are afraid of what will happen if we ever find out.

ETHAN. Why?

DEREK. Well. *What would we do if we ever found out?* Some truth that big? The earth is flat. Think about that. What is the first thing you would do if you found out that something so basically true is in fact one hundred percent false? I'd have a drink. No! I wouldn't! I'm not drinking anymore! Ever! Stop making fun of me!

> (**ETHAN** *laughs;* **DEREK** *is charming when he's drunk.*)

> (*A young man,* **CURT**, *and a young woman,* **HALEY**, *enter. They are speaking to each other.*)

HALEY. ...But it's hilarious that he doesn't know it's her the entire time.

CURT. But no, don't you think he *does* know? I think that's part of the gag.

HALEY. Absolutely not, no, the plot *hinges* on his not knowing that the woman in his house is the same woman he met on the ship.

CURT. (*To* **DEREK**.) Oh, hey, Derek. And...uhhh...

ETHAN. Ethan.

CURT. Ethan, right. This is Haley. We met today. She knows all these old movies that I know – I thought I was the only one.

HALEY. Hello.

CURT. I think I'm in love with her.

> (*Awkward silence.*)

DEREK. Hi, Haley.

HALEY. What are you guys doing?

ETHAN. Discussing whether or not the earth is flat.

HALEY. Hysterical.

CURT. I know it's crazy, but I really think I love her.

HALEY. We just met today.

CURT. I know, but...don't you feel it? Love at first sight? Don't you?

HALEY. I do. I do, but maybe let's not talk about it. Maybe it's a spell that can be broken if you speak it out loud.
(*To* **ETHAN** *and* **DEREK**.) He's sweet, right? You spend all this time alone growing up watching Barbara Stanwyck movies and you don't realize that someone else is doing

the exact same thing, and that you'll meet him one day, and that he'll be this cute, and straight – you're straight, right?

CURT. Yeah. Yeah. Yes. Yes, I am.

HALEY. Sweet.

> (*To* **ETHAN** *and* **DEREK**.) I feel like I've landed in Oz, or something. I guess you just never know.

CURT. (*To* **HALEY**.) I have *Double Indemnity* on my phone. Should we go watch it in my room?

HALEY. *There's a speed limit in this state, Mr. Neff. Forty-five miles an hour.*

CURT. *How fast was I going, officer?*

HALEY. *I'd say around ninety.*

CURT. *Suppose you get down off your motorcycle and give me a ticket.*

HALEY. *Suppose I let you off with a warning this time.*

CURT. *Suppose it doesn't take.*

HALEY. *Suppose I have to whack you over the knuckles.*

CURT. *Suppose I bust out crying and put my head on your shoulder.*

HALEY. *Suppose you try putting it on my husband's shoulder.*

CURT. *That tears it.*

> (*They go.*)

ETHAN. So why don't we fall off the edge? If it's flat.

DEREK. (*Excited.*) I know the answer: *Antarctica.*

ETHAN. Wow you said *that* without slurring...

DEREK. Told you! No one ever knew I was drunk.

ETHAN. We don't fall off because of Antarctica?

DEREK. Ancartita is actually all around us – it's the edge of the world in all directions. Like the rim of a gl– (*Hiccup.*) –*ass.* We can't fall off the edge 'cause we have never even gotten near to it.

ETHAN. Because of Antarctica?

DEREK. Yeah. It's a wall of ice. No one knows how wide it is.

ETHAN. Then what's above us?

DEREK. Dome.

ETHAN. And what's below us?

DEREK. Pillars.

ETHAN. And the sun?

DEREK. Goes like this.

> *(Demonstrates an object passing in a circular pattern above a flat, plate-like Earth.)*

It's under the dome with us.

ETHAN. *(Laughs.)* You're making this up.

DEREK. Nope. Nope. Nope. Lots of people... *(Hiccup.)* ...believe this.

ETHAN. And who put the sun under the dome for us?

DEREK. God.

ETHAN. And why?

DEREK. That. Is. The. Question.

ETHAN. *(Silent for a moment.)* Huh.

DEREK. I know.

ETHAN. But like space and the moon and the stars. Gravity. This was all figured out hundreds and hundreds of years ago.

DEREK. Or was it?

ETHAN. I think it *was*.

> *(Silence.)*

Derek?

DEREK. Yes?

ETHAN. Do you believe the earth is flat?

DEREK. No. I'm not stupid.

ETHAN. Just checking.

DEREK. I'm sorry about your brother.

> *(**ETHAN** doesn't answer.)*

I don't want you to leave.

ETHAN. I'll be back.

DEREK. Then why are you taking all of your stuff?

ETHAN. Oh. I don't know, I got so confused.

DEREK. I'm not going to drink anymore. I promise.

ETHAN. You don't have to make that promise. You're in college.

DEREK. No. No. Look what it does. Look. There's a wall between us, and I can't get to you, and I really want to. That's all it does. Keeps me from you. Antarctica! I vow. I'm not drinking ever again. Ever. I vow. For you. For your *brother*. I can do that.

ETHAN. You're fine, you didn't do anything wrong.

DEREK. You need to get to the airport.

ETHAN. I know. I don't want to move. I like this better than...

DEREK. Look. E is F. Earth is Flat. Earth is Fucked. Ethan is Farewell. Everything is Fading. Everyone is Freaking out. Everything isn't Fine.

ETHAN. Oh, Derek.

DEREK. I'm sorry. I'm sorry. Antarctica. I'm sorry.

> (**DEREK** *is passed out.*)
>
> (**ETHAN** *helps get* **DEREK** *to his feet. He takes him into 802.*)
>
> (**ETHAN** *pushes the boxes toward the elevator.*)
>
> (*This is ridiculous.*)
>
> (*He pushes them into the lounge.*)
>
> (*He fishes a piece of paper out of his backpack, and a Sharpie.*)
>
> (*He writes something on the piece of paper – finds a push pin from someone's cork board and pins the paper to the lounge door.*)
>
> (*The piece of paper reads: Free stuff.*)
>
> (*He goes.*)

Scene Three
Delayed

(ETHAN is back home in Denver.)

(He is leaning over the sink in the small bathroom of his childhood home.)

(His sister, JENNIFER, is dyeing his hair.)

JENNIFER. If you were that upset about it, we should have done this a week ago, *before* the funeral.

ETHAN. I know, I know. You're right. I don't know why I let you talk me into it in the first place.

JENNIFER. You're welcome. And also, *screw* Uncle Jim. He's a hick. Since when is he the arbiter of good taste? Does he *look* in the mirror? Ever? Those clothes – he looks like...well, what he *is*...a straight, old know-it-all farmer who's *never left Colorado. He* gets to give fashion advice?

ETHAN. I know, I know.

JENNIFER. I loved your purple hair. Now you'll be just like everyone else.

(She shudders at this thought.)

How did he say it?

ETHAN. *(Sighs.)* "Who do you think you are, showing up to your brother's funeral looking like a circus clown? I'm ashamed of you."

JENNIFER. Whatever. *Jeremy* liked your hair. So.

ETHAN. He did. The day I left for school – did you hear him say this? – he was like, "Of course the first Jeffrey kid to go to college has purple hair. It's cool, Ethan." And he was rubbing my head, I worried my hair would stain his leather gloves.

JENNIFER. You know Uncle Jim hit his new girlfriend, right? Nobody *talks* about it, but he did. Also, it's not like you dyed your hair *specifically for your brother's funeral.* You were living your life and you didn't know that your brother was going to...

(Gets a little choked up.) ...Whatever, I don't want to talk about Uncle Jim anymore.

(Silence as she focuses on her task.)

Is this dye too dark? *That* might be cool, actually. Should we go jet black? Maybe shave half of your head? No, just the dye.

ETHAN. Dye. Die. Dye. Die. Dye.

JENNIFER. Is Mom talking to you, yet?

*(**JENNIFER** looks under the sink for a towel.)*

ETHAN. She said she will once I dye.

JENNIFER. Christ on a pogo stick!

ETHAN. *What?*

*(**JENNIFER** pulls out a bottle of liquor from under the sink.)*

I thought it was pills these days?

JENNIFER. Gotta wash it down with something.

(She dumps it down the drain.)

Someone at the funeral, I think she's like the mom of one of Jeremy's friends, asked me if he was drunk when his motorcycle flipped, and I was like, "You don't know what you're effing talking about, lady. He never touched the stuff. He was like an eagle out there soaring above the earth and you couldn't even touch his beauty," and I just unloaded on her in this psychotic metaphor about Jeremy being an eagle and then a god and then a mountain and then a guitar, I don't know, she really *pushed my button*...

(She gets a little choked up and then laughs.)

...it was hilarious, actually, I was screaming at this poor woman, "He was a *god*, he was *clean. You* may choke down that poison, lady, but *he*, he..."

*(Suddenly, **JENNIFER** starts crying. Sad about Jeremy. **ETHAN** just lets her. It's quiet and just sad. She takes a second to pull herself together.)*

ETHAN. I know.

(*Beat.*)

(*Looking around.*) I had this feeling, when I left, that I was never going to come back here. Never. Never.

JENNIFER. Gee, thanks.

ETHAN. Well. Me and Mom.

(*Looks around.*)

It's like I just woke up, and Cincinnati wasn't even real. *I had the most wonderful dream, and* you *weren't there, and* you *weren't there, and* you *weren't there.*

(*This makes* **JENNIFER** *laugh.*)

When do you go back to school? Surely you're not allowed to miss two full weeks of the eleventh grade, even when your brother dies.

(*Silence.*)

JENNIFER. (*Sigh. Then, confidently, ready for an argument.*) I'm going to drop out. Of high school.

ETHAN. What? Why?

(*Fatherly.*) No.

JENNIFER. I don't need it.

ETHAN. Of course you need it. Jennifer.

JENNIFER. Ugh. Okay, look: I'm smarter than *every single one* of my teachers. I don't mean that as obnoxious teenage hyperbole, I am *actually* smarter than they are. I *correct* them in class. All the time. They are afraid of me – like, I don't do my homework, *ever*, and they still give me passing grades. Because they know I'm smarter than they are.

ETHAN. Jennifer – (*Sighs.*)

JENNIFER. No, I'm not a jerk to them, I don't bully them. I talk to them, after school. Like, I'll go into Mr. Philippe's class, after school, and just have an *adult* conversation with him about history. Isn't that the point, anyway? That we learn how to be *adults* in this world, in this society? I know how to do that. I read *a lot*, you know that. I read books that are more sophisticated than textbooks. I don't need to learn how to be engaged with the world, *I am engaged with the world.* I hate sitting in class because everyone else, I'm sorry to say, is an *idiot.* They cannot answer questions, they cannot string words together into nice, shiny little sentences. They are dullards. High school is for dullards.

ETHAN. So why drop out if it's so easy and you're so good at it? Stay and get good grades and get into a great college.

JENNIFER. College! High school, the sequel! Nope.

ETHAN. College is great.

JENNIFER. How would you know?

ETHAN. Jennifer, listen to me. You're finishing high school, and then going to college.

JENNIFER. Do you know I'm the *manager* now, at the Lube and Dash? The *manager.* I am sixteen years old, and I am *running* the place. Like, middle-aged men report to me. I don't know anything about cars! And I'm the manager now. They love me.

ETHAN. So you're going to drop out of school to work at the auto supply store? Called the *Lube. And. Dash*?

JENNIFER. No! Please! I'm just saying, I know how to be an adult in this world and the thought of one more year of high school *after* this year is enough to make me want to give myself a frontal lobotomy. They are all idiots!

ETHAN. And you think being a "high school dropout" is *not* going to make *you* look like an idiot.

JENNIFER. After five minutes of conversation, people will *know* that I'm not an idiot.

ETHAN. This is a really shitty time, Jennifer, to be doing this! Jesus Christ. Please tell me you haven't said this to your mother? While she's doped up and melting with grief. Honestly, Jennifer. What is wrong with you?

JENNIFER. What's wrong with *you*, old man? Suddenly you're on *her* side?
(*Mocking him.*) *You're finishing high school and you're going to college.* You sound like everyone else.

ETHAN. Who? Who else have you...

JENNIFER. Anyone. Everyone. People who say things like *You're finishing high school and you're going to college.* I don't want to go to college. I'm not going. I don't want to go to effing High School anymore, I'm not going. You can make up your own rules in this lifetime. You can dye your hair purple if you want. Well, not *you*, I guess.

(Silence.)

All of those idiots will *hug* me now.

They'll want to have quiet conversations about Jeremy, and tell me little anecdotes about Jeremy, and...ugh... about some nice thing he said to them, or did for them. I can't bear it. I actually *cannot* bear it. And I'm not asking your permission, I'm just letting you know.

(Silence.)

(Muttering to herself.)

(Then, suddenly exploding.) Seven hundred dollars! Is how much I've managed to save already. Seven hundred dollars. And that's *AFTER* buying my own clothes, buying a shitty old used car, paying for my own meals every day – I don't ask Mom for *anything*. In fact, she borrows money from me. But I don't care. I like taking care of myself, and of other people, and I can. I pay for everything AND I've managed to save seven hundred dollars. And don't tell me life is not about money because I know that already, having grown up in a house with *no money at effing all*, but *if you think about it*, life *is* about money, because if you *don't have money*, then your life is *only about making enough money to live*. So you *need* money if you want to have the luxury of your life *not* being about money. I'm actually, like, ten steps ahead of most adults at this point.

(Silence.)

(The hair dyeing is done. Because of the tension in the room, they finish the last bits – the drying, the combing – in silence.)

(**JENNIFER** *and* **ETHAN** *contemplate the results in the mirror.*)

You look like Dad.

ETHAN. Jesus. I really do.

JENNIFER. Hey, Dad, Mom won't get out of bed. What should we do? I think she needs a refill of Klonopin, can you get it from the pharmacy – they won't give it to a sixteen-year-old high school dropout like me.

ETHAN. You're not funny.

JENNIFER. I'm not joking.

What do you say, Dad? Can you come back home to us, old man, and do all the things that dads are supposed to do? I think Mom might be down for the count with this one and I can't be here alone with her. I can't. I can't do it.

(**ETHAN** *is upset by this.*)

I'll stick it out, the eleventh grade, if you stay.

(*Silence.*)

Seriously, Ethan, I think the big bad wolf might blow our little house-of-twigs over. Can you stay and help us fight him off?

ETHAN. Who's the big bad wolf?

JENNIFER. Life. Death. Whatever.

(*She looks at him intensely in the mirror.*)

You really do look like Dad.

(**ETHAN** *looks in the mirror and sighs.*)

Scene Four
The Post

*(**ETHAN** is still at his home in Colorado.)*

(He is on the sofa.)

(A sudden pounding on the door.)

ETHAN. Hello?

JENNIFER. *(Outside.)* Can you open the door?

ETHAN. It's open!

JENNIFER. I know but...can you...?

ETHAN. It should be unlocked!

JENNIFER. Would you just...believe me when I say I need your help. God!

ETHAN. *(Getting up to open the door.)* Sorry. Coming.

(He opens the door.)

*(There is **JENNIFER**, holding two boxes and standing amid many, many more.)*

(These are Ethan's boxes from college.)

ETHAN. Holy...!

JENNIFER. FedEx guy just...what is all this stuff?

ETHAN. Here...

(Helps her bring them in.)

...

JENNIFER. What is all this?

ETHAN. Oh, god. I can't shake these things!

JENNIFER. *(Opening a box.)* You took all of this to college?

ETHAN. I didn't think I'd be back.

JENNIFER. There's a letter.

ETHAN. *(Opening, smiles.)* It's from Derek. My...roommate.

JENNIFER. *(Gasp.)* You! Just got little hearts for eyes!

ETHAN. Shut up.

JENNIFER. *Derek.* Ooh – you love your roommate. *Awkward.*

ETHAN. He's not my roommate, I don't even know him. Really.

JENNIFER. But you don't deny loving him?

ETHAN. I was there for one night.

JENNIFER. Was it a magical night?

ETHAN. Shut up. He's straight.

JENNIFER. Really straight or like college-freshman straight?

ETHAN. Really straight.

JENNIFER. *(Re: letter.)* What's it say?

ETHAN. *(Reading.)* It's personal.

JENNIFER. *"Dear Ethan, please do hurry back. I realize that I can't live without you. I look at your empty bed and weep till dawn. I've broken up with Genevieve, it's time I faced the truth. I love you. Here are your things, I've smelled each item trying to conjure our one, transformative evening together, but to no avail. I couldn't bear to keep them as a pale simulacrum of dearest you. Return or forget me forever."*

ETHAN. Are you done?

JENNIFER. *"PS: I think I'm pregnant."*

ETHAN. I hate you.

JENNIFER. But you love Derek.

ETHAN. No. It's not like that. He's cool.

JENNIFER. Is he cute?

ETHAN. Beyond.

JENNIFER. That letter is like ten pages long! There is no way he's straight.

ETHAN. He's straight, he's just sophisticated. Leave me alone so I can read this. Don't you have homework?

JENNIFER. Yes, Dad. I have to finish my social studies paper on Prohibition. Just so you know, that's how I'm spending my evening. Isn't that a great use of my life? Homework.

ETHAN. You'll thank me.

JENNIFER. Oh, Dad, don't let Mom see the letter from your mistress, there.

(She goes.)

(**ETHAN** *reads the letter.*)

(**DEREK** *appears and speaks what* **ETHAN** *is reading.*)

DEREK. Ethan! Here's all your shit! Ha, just kidding. But I hope it gets to you. I found your address written on the side of one of the boxes – I hope it's your address. It says DENVER at least, and I figured that DENVER is a small enough little village that even if this wasn't your address anyone who got it would all know where you lived.

I woke up the morning after you left completely hungover and really embarrassed by how I behaved. I'm sorry. Was I obnoxious? Horrible.

Are you doing okay? I hope so, pal.

I was walking to breakfast when I saw your FREE STUFF sign – you are crazy! I immediately grabbed all of the boxes – one of them had been opened, so I don't know if this is *everything*, but here is what I found! These boxes sat on your bed for a while until I finally had to make peace with the fact that you weren't coming back.

I don't have your phone number and I don't have Facebook or anything like that – Oh, man! You didn't even get to hear my lengthy dissertation on the evils of social media!

(Laughs.)

Lucky you. So here is a (long) handwritten letter. Isn't that kinda romantic and old-school? A letter from Ohio. I feel like a homestead wife – sending news back East.

(Re: Jeremy.) How are you doing?

I figure you're sad to be away from college, even though your mom is probably making you Christmas tree cookies sprinkled with mood-stabilizers every day, so, as your roommate, and best-college-friend, I decided that it's my duty to fill you in on all that's been happening here.

The eighth floor is kinda party central of the dorm. The lounge is always full of passed-out freshmen, garbage, vomit, it's...it smells so bad on this floor. I have burned through all but two of my candles, and probably those, also, by the time you get this.

There was a giant inflatable stick of deodorant in the center of the campus. I guess, like, the deodorant company was giving away free samples and the college was okay with them advertising like that. There's always some company trying to sell us crap. I kinda forget we're here to go to class sometimes.

I have a hazy memory of the night before you left – was I lying on the floor talking about how the Earth is Flat? I was, wasn't I?

ETHAN. Yes.

DEREK. Agh! I am insane. I'm sorry I subjected you to that. You didn't really get the chance to know me – though don't you feel like we instantly clicked? When was making a friend ever that easy? I think I brought up the *Earth is Flat* thing because it is part of my singular obsession in life: I am singularly obsessed with people who are singularly obsessed. For example: I don't really know the *Star Wars* movies that well – I saw them when I was a kid, so I've *seen* them, but I don't *know* them, you know? – but I am fascinated by people who are obsessed with those films. I could watch hours and hours of YouTube videos where people dig into the minutiae of those films. Same with conspiracy theorists. I spend – WASTE! – so much time watching videos that these people.

Lately I've discovered this whole group of Flat Earthers (that's what they call themselves) on YouTube. It's this *giant* conspiracy theory – and trust me, all of this is leading to a POINT that has to do with college life here in Cincinnati, I promise – it's this conspiracy theory wherein the government, of course, is lying to us about the earth's being a globe. It's a lie! A big lie propagated by NASA and "the Elite" to...I don't know, keep us zombified sheep from learning the truth. I can't stop watching. Oh, and religious fanatics. I love them, too. Anyone who has grabbed onto the psychological electric fence of some crazy conspiracy and can't let go. But I'm really into the Flat Earth conspiracy people right now. God, is this boring? I remember once a friend of mine kept going on and on in this endless story about the airport losing his luggage and it was unbearable. Wonder whatever happened to that guy?

(**ETHAN** *laughs, blushes.*)

Anyway, I have a favorite Flat Earther. Her name is Shelley. She puts up these three hour (Three Hour!) videos where she interviews other Flat Earthers (That name! So dumb! Oh, want to know another dumb word I recently heard? It's referencing an emerging musical style: Folktronica. Barf!) and I have watched all twenty-five of her three-hour videos. That's Seventy-Five hours of just watching Shelley and her myopic obsession with the Flat Earth. Homework? What homework?

Well, here is the BIG POINT of all of this. SHE GOES TO SCHOOL here! Can you believe it?! She is a grad student at the university. She's a little older than us. Hot. Anyway, I saw her on the campus and I was star-struck. She could've been standing next to Jennifer Lawrence and the entire cast of *Harry Potter*, it wouldn't have mattered, I would have wanted to meet Shelley. She's sexy. But crazy. I'd want to kiss her. But also NOT kiss her. She makes me feel all sorts of things. Anyway, I'm crazy about her videos and now I'm obsessed with knowing she goes to school here. I've not, like, *looked* for her, or anything, I don't ever want to meet her. I don't think. But I also want to marry her. This is a problem.

(**JENNIFER** *walks through the room.*)

JENNIFER. Oh. My. God. You have pure elation on your face. What is he saying?!

ETHAN. Go away!

JENNIFER. Oooooooohhhhhhh.

(She goes.)

*(**ETHAN** goes back to reading the letter.)*

ETHAN. *(Reading.)* I don't ever want to meet her. I don't think. But I also want to marry her. This is a problem.

DEREK. So here's what I think we should do right now.

Let's hang out, even though I'm not there.

Imagine that I am there.

Imagine that you've come into our room, 802, you've had a busy day of classes – I don't even know what your major is! – and you've stepped over the drunk and vomit-smeared blonde kid from 814 – he's a disaster, that kid – and you've entered our clean and peaceful room. It smells like apple pie – that's the candle I've got burning. I say: Ethan! I've got to show you something. Get your computer. And you do. You get your computer – get your computer now, play along in this fantasy. Have you got your computer, Ethan? I'll wait.

Good. You've got your computer. I say: Go to YouTube. (Go to YouTube!) I say: Type in Flat Earth Whole Enchilada, that's the name of her show.

ETHAN. *(Has gotten his computer, typing.)* Flat Earth Whole Enchilada.

DEREK. And I say: See that video that's called, "Flat Earth Whole Enchilada show number eighteen, with guest Jeremy Calwirth"? – Jeremy, wasn't that your brother's name, I seem to remember that – Click on that one.

ETHAN. *(Does.)* Okay.

DEREK. Now, let's watch this together. Press play – now!

ETHAN. *(He does.)* Oh, Derek.

(He can't breathe, this is so romantic.)

(Suddenly, a striking young **WOMAN** *appears. She is the YouTube video that* **DEREK** *and* **ETHAN** *are watching. This is* **SHELLEY**.*)*

SHELLEY. Hello, and welcome to "Flat Earth Whole Enchilada," the show where we discuss the most vital issue of our day – you guessed it, the Flat Earth.

DEREK. Isn't she gorgeous? I know you're...but you can admit, she's hot.

ETHAN. Whatever.

SHELLEY. My guest today is Jeremy Calwirth.

JEREMY CALWIRTH. Hi, Shelley.

SHELLEY. Jeremy has been making Flat Earth videos for a couple of years now.

JEREMY CALWIRTH. That's right, Shelley, the world is finally starting to catch up.

SHELLEY. To *wake* up!

JEREMY CALWIRTH. That's right, exactly. It's about time! Global Alarm Clock!

SHELLEY. Only *non-global.*

JEREMY CALWIRTH. Oh, Shelley. Touché.

DEREK. He is so in love with her. Watch this, watch this part right at forty-five seconds, how he looks at her.

(We see **JEREMY** *give* **SHELLEY** *a lecherous ogle.)*

*(***ETHAN** *laughs.)*

Did you see that?

ETHAN. Yes, yes!

SHELLEY.

What do you have for us today, Jeremy?	**DEREK.**
Any new exciting news in the world of –	Wait! Wait! Go back, we have to watch that again. Go back.

*(***ETHAN** *goes back ten seconds.)*

DEREK. You can see it on his lips: *Marry me, Shelley.*

(**ETHAN** *plays the part again.*)

JEREMY CALWIRTH. That's right, exactly. It's about time! Global Alarm Clock!

SHELLEY. Only *non-global*.

JEREMY CALWIRTH. Oh, Shelley. Touché.

(*Creepy look from* **JEREMY** *to* **SHELLEY**.)

DEREK. Did you see that! EFFING HILARIOUS!!

SHELLEY.	**DEREK.**
Any new exciting news in the world of –	He does this on every episode – I need to see it one more time.

(**ETHAN** *plays it again.*)

SHELLEY. Only *non-global*.

JEREMY CALWIRTH. Oh, Shelley. Touché.

(*Creepy look from* **JEREMY**. *The* **BOYS** *laugh.*)

SHELLEY. Any new exciting news in the world of Flat Earth?

DEREK. They are – /

JEREMY CALWIRTH. Ohhh, Shelley... /

DEREK. Singularly...oh, did you hear that?! / The way he said her name?

JEREMY CALWIRTH. ...Do I ever.

DEREK. I get it, though, she's sexy as anything.

SHELLEY. Well, I can't wait to hear what news you have.

DEREK. Okay, now, listen to this. Doesn't he look like our weird neighbor James?

JEREMY CALWIRTH. So, here's something interesting that our YouTube friend DropintheBucketofBullshit42 has been vlogging about: Did you know, Shelley, did you *know*... that there is not one single image from NASA of planet Earth? Not ONE.

SHELLEY. I did know that, but maybe our viewers don't know. What Jeremy is referring to is the fact that every photo of the earth that NASA puts out is labeled in very small letters as a "composite photo," meaning that it's partially or completely rendered by an artist and not, as you are led to believe, a simple snapshot of the earth like...like...

JEREMY CALWIRTH. Like the astronaut has an iPhone and is just snapping a picture from space. There is no space! You can't get to space! There is a dome above us – the International Space Station is...I don't know, some studio in Burbank. A joke!

SHELLEY. And do you know how they make the astronauts appear to be weightless?

JEREMY CALWIRTH. Of course. They film a lot underwater, but also just green screen and ropes.

DEREK. Isn't this fascinating?

ETHAN. Yes.

DEREK. I hope you said yes.

ETHAN. I did say yes, I did!

SHELLEY. Jeremy. Can I say...

JEREMY CALWIRTH. Sure, Shelley, anything.

SHELLEY. I know we want the whole world to wake up to this, but...I kind of enjoy our secret society.

DEREK. I love this part.

JEREMY CALWIRTH. Secret society?

SHELLEY. Well, you know, it's a little club at this point. Exclusive. Those of us who know the truth.

JEREMY CALWIRTH. Are you calling us the *elite*, Shelley?

SHELLEY. *(Laughs.)* No. I just. I don't have many friends in the matrix-world, because of this. Anymore. But I have better friends now. I have *true* friends in the *truth*.

JEREMY CALWIRTH. Aww, Shelley, I'm your friend.

SHELLEY. You are. You are my friend.

DEREK. Look how sad he is. At the word *friend*.

SHELLEY. And I'm just so grateful to this community, that's all. I've really found...my people. At last, the Flat Earthers have embraced me.

JEREMY CALWIRTH. Oh, Shelley. We love you.

(**DEREK** *laughs.*)

SHELLEY. Anyway. Just feeling...

DEREK. PS, Ethan, look at the time-remaining counter at the bottom of the screen. Two Hours and Forty-Seven Minutes! They just go round and round like this. I love it.

JEREMY CALWIRTH. It's a good feeling. I agree.

SHELLEY.

SHELLEY.	**DEREK.**
Does it make you wonder, Jeremy my friend, just how many people know for a fact what the truth is? How deep does this go? And why don't people see what is just so obvious, so *obviously* right there in front of them. It's there in writing, even, *composite* photo. But no one pays attention. Sad.	This is what I do. Now you know. I watch people like this. For hours. So if you were here, I'd no doubt have you watching this with me. For hours. You'd be trapped! It's nice, isn't it?

ETHAN.

Yes. Yes.

DEREK.

Come back. Come back and let me trap you beside me, force you to watch more...

(**JENNIFER** *has entered, unnoticed.*)

JENNIFER. What are you watching?

ETHAN. Nothing. (*Closes it like it's pornography.*)

JENNIFER. Mom says you should, how did she put it?

(*Imitates a drugged-up person slurring something incomprehensible.*)

ETHAN. What does that mean?

JENNIFER. I have no idea. But she handed me this – looks like a list of chores for you to do. Quick warning, number three is a bit overwhelming: "Clean up this mess." Jesus Christ, your *eyes*.

ETHAN. What?

JENNIFER. I don't know. You just look...so *happy*. And, like, the *opposite* at the same time.

ETHAN. Oh. Just. I. Derek. I mean. He's. So. And. I'm. I think I. I shouldn't have. I mean, I'm. What am I doing? Home? I should...

> *(Looks at the list of chores.)*

> *(Looks at the letter from Derek.)*

I *am*. So happy.

> *(Looks at the list of chores.)*

And the opposite.

At the same time.

JENNIFER. You're leaving, aren't you?

> *(Silence.)*

> *(Blackout.)*

End of Act One

ACT TWO

Scene Five
Arrival Pt. 2

(It is January. ETHAN is back at the university.)

(We are in the dorm hallway once again.)

(DEREK has a little bottle of champagne with glasses and a WELCOME BACK, ETHAN banner hanging.)

(DEREK pops the champagne! Throws a little confetti.)

DEREK. *(Making a speech.)* I decided that it really makes more sense to start school in the new year, anyway, so let's just call this the first day of college. The last few months have passed in an actual blink – we've never left this hallway, you and I, we're still just meeting, and just getting started. Right where we left off. Welcome back, dear Ethan. College without a roommate, f.y.i., is for the birds.

ETHAN. Yay. Aww. Derek, thank you.

> *(They toast.)*

What is this?

DEREK. It's sparkling cider. I'm on the wagon. Believe it or not.

> *(ETHAN is not sure how to respond.)*

After that night, when I was so...that was the moment.

> *(Beat.)*

What a nerd? I know.

ETHAN. No, the opposite. I was thinking the opposite.

DEREK. Cheers.

ETHAN. Cheers.

> *(They drink.)*
>
> *(**DEREK** holds up a bowl of chips...)*

DEREK. The chips you like!

> *(**ETHAN** smiles.)*

I'm even wearing the same shirt I wore the day we met here. I love ceremonies. I love superstition. Catholic. Vestments. Robes. Magic underwear. All that. The clothes make the man. You are what you wear. Or is it eat? Maybe she's born with it, maybe it's Maybelline. You know what I'm saying.

ETHAN. I played Cards Against Humanity with my sister, back home – my favorite answer ever was: Maybe she's born with it, maybe it's horse meat.

> *(They laugh.)*
>
> *(Suddenly, the **GUY** who looks like Ethan's brother walks by, just as before.)*

(Startled, scared.) Look.

DEREK. What?

ETHAN. It's that guy again. That guy who looks like my brother.

DEREK. Him?

ETHAN. Yup.

> *(They watch.)*

It's alarming. He looks *exactly* like him. Exactly.

> *(Silence.)*
>
> *(Slightly awkward. **ETHAN** is upset.)*

DEREK. I'm sorry.

ETHAN. It hits me just like that. He'll just be there, suddenly, in my mind. But that guy actually looks just like him.

DEREK. *(Not sure what to say.)* Can I... I don't know exactly what to say.

ETHAN. I feel like, I want to talk about him but I know it just makes people sad and uncomfortable. And after a while it's just a bit of a drain, so...

DEREK. You can talk about him with me. You can talk about him all you want.

ETHAN. His funeral was like – have you ever, in adding up money or something good, ever got the decimal point wrong? And suddenly, for a moment, you have so much more than you thought? But then you realize that you just got the math wrong, and you're actually at a deficit? That's how his funeral felt – the exact moment where we all realized that this Jeremy-sized surplus wasn't correct, and now we were back to operating at a deficit. That sounds so bleak, but...

DEREK. Mmm-hmm.

ETHAN. The more I talk about him in the past tense, the more he becomes the past tense.

> (**ETHAN** *looks at* **DEREK**. *Silence.*)

Thank you.

> *(Silence.)*

For...

> *(Silence.)*

What is the opposite of a nerd?

DEREK. I don't know, is this a joke?

ETHAN. You said you were a nerd earlier, and I said, "No, you're the opposite." I was just thinking *what is the opposite of a nerd.*

DEREK. Oh. Ha.

ETHAN. 'Cause that's what you are.

DEREK. Oh. Yeah? Thanks.

ETHAN. Yeah. That's what you are.

DEREK. Huh. Cool. I'm glad you're back.

ETHAN. Yeah.

> (**ETHAN** *leans in and kisses* **DEREK. DEREK**
> *doesn't pull away quickly or rudely, but he*
> *is clearly not interested in the kiss, so he does*
> *pull away, not wanting to hurt or embarrass*
> **ETHAN.***)*

DEREK. Umm...

ETHAN. That was nice.

DEREK. Ethan? I'm...

ETHAN. What?

DEREK. You know I'm...

> (**ETHAN** *is silent.*)

You know I'm not that... I'm not...

ETHAN. Maybe...

> (**ETHAN** *leans in for another kiss; this time*
> **DEREK** *pulls away more sharply.*)

DEREK. Ethan. Come on. Don't...

ETHAN. I...

> (*Awkward silence.*)

DEREK. I don't care that you are, but I'm just...not.

ETHAN. Oh, god.

DEREK. It's okay – don't...

ETHAN. Oh my god.

DEREK. No, it's... I get it, I know. I know...feelings, like, it's
hard to...sometimes...

ETHAN. I'm sorry. I'm so embarrassed.

DEREK. No, you don't have to. It's confusing, I'm sure, I
know, it's okay...

ETHAN. I guess I got this idea...oh, my god...that you...

DEREK. Look, it doesn't change anything, it's okay...

ETHAN. It's...

DEREK. I'm not upset.

ETHAN. ...Humiliating.

DEREK. It's not, it's... Can I...?

> (**ETHAN** *starts eating the chips. He won't look at* **DEREK**.)

Look, let me tell you... I used to fool around with my neighbor, when I was younger, and like, it wasn't a big deal, I don't... He turned out gay and I turned out straight, and we were friends, we're *still* friendly, I don't have... Oh, man, I'm just remembering, you would have loved this. We used to have sleepovers at his house and we'd spend all this time in his basement, and, listen to this, this was his basement: one side was just stacks and stacks and stacks of his dad's porno magazines and the other side was stacks of his mom's Mary Kay supplies. She sold to all the neighbor ladies. Isn't that funny? We would hide out down there and look at EVERY magazine, and we'd like...have sex. It wasn't...

> (**ETHAN** *puts too many chips into his mouth.*)
>
> (*He's chewing in awkward silence, but then something changes.*)
>
> (*He turns away from* **DEREK**.)
>
> (*Something is wrong.*)

Ethan, you okay?

> (**ETHAN** *gestures that he is fine, but it becomes apparent that he is choking on the chips.*)

Ethan? Are you okay?

> (**ETHAN** *gestures again that he is fine.*)
>
> (*Only suddenly he is not fine.*)
>
> (*He starts panicking – grabbing at his throat.*)
>
> (*He is choking.*)
>
> (*He can't breathe.*)
>
> (**DEREK** *instantly grabs him, turns him, and gives him the Heimlich maneuver.*)
>
> (*It works.*)

(**ETHAN** *spits out the chips.*)

(*He coughs and gasps.*)

ETHAN. I couldn't breathe. I couldn't breathe.

DEREK. You're okay, now. It's okay. Here, drink this.

(**DEREK** *hands* **ETHAN** *the sparkling drink.*)

(**ETHAN** *drinks. He is still trying to actually catch his breath.*)

ETHAN. I couldn't breathe.

(*After a moment, he calms. There is tension.*)

I'm so embarrassed to be alive right now. I can't look at you. I'm shaking.

DEREK. That was intense. You wanna go in the room and lie down?

ETHAN. I'm gonna... I'm gonna...

(**ETHAN** *runs off.* **DEREK** *calls after him:*)

DEREK. Ethan! Don't be...! Where are you going – Ethan!!

(**ETHAN** *doesn't respond, but rather keeps walking.*)

Scene Six
Detour

(**ETHAN** *is in the university library.*)

(*He sits at a table, puts his head down.*)

(*There is a chair pulled out next to him and a stack of books; clearly, someone is sitting here, they are just momentarily absent.*)

(*Sure enough, a* **WOMAN** *appears to claim the open seat.*)

(*It is none other than* **SHELLEY**, *the Flat Earth conspiracy theorist from YouTube.*)

SHELLEY. Hello? Are you sick?

ETHAN. (*Not lifting his head.*) No.

SHELLEY. Do you need me to get help?

ETHAN. (*Doesn't lift his head until indicated.*) No.

SHELLEY. Okay. Do you mind maybe scooching down a bit – I...?

(**ETHAN** *scooches.*)

ETHAN. Sorry.

SHELLEY. Are you drunk?

ETHAN. No. Just recently nearly dead.

(*She sits and reads/works.*)

(**ETHAN** *keeps his head on the table.*)

SHELLEY. Maybe you could nap in your dorm room? It's a little aggressive to do it at the library.

ETHAN. I don't have anywhere to go.

SHELLEY. Do you go to school here?

ETHAN. Yes. No. Yes. I don't know. I keep trying to.

SHELLEY. Is this a cry for attention?

(*Silence.*)

ETHAN. No.

(*Silence.*)

ETHAN. I tried to kiss someone and...they didn't want me to...

SHELLEY. Oh, dear.

ETHAN. I thought, in that moment, I would die of humiliation, but then I...choked on some chips, and actually nearly died. To be denied a kiss. Then to lie dead at his feet. How mortifying. He had to give me the Heimlich maneuver. Oh. My. God.

SHELLEY. You choked? Are you okay?

ETHAN. He saved my life. Whyyyyy?

SHELLEY. Wow. Like, the actual Heimlich maneuver? I've never known anyone who needed the Heimlich maneuver, it's just a bad eighties PSA in my mind.

ETHAN. It works. I can testify. I wish he would have let me die.

SHELLEY. Don't say that. You pass this way but once. Once! Don't wish it away.

    (Silence.)

Was it a friend you tried to kiss? That happened to me just recently. Guy I work with, Jeremy, tried to kiss me. Not. Cool.

ETHAN. It was my roommate.

SHELLEY. You tried to kiss your *roommate*?

ETHAN. I know. I know.

SHELLEY. I think that's like page one in the dorm rulebook. It just says: don't.

ETHAN. Your voice sounds very familiar to me, do I know you?

SHELLEY. I don't know. Maybe.

ETHAN. Probably not, I just started school here. For the second time.

SHELLEY. Welcome. Back.

ETHAN. It's not what I thought it would be. At all.

SHELLEY. Well, nothing is.

ETHAN. I came to school, before, and then a terrible thing happened and I had to leave. And now I'm back, and what I thought I was coming back to is not at all what's here.

SHELLEY. Yup, that's about right. Sounds like maybe you're waking up, that's all. Seeing the illusion. I woke up not so long ago.

ETHAN. What do you mean?

SHELLEY. Most people are sleepwalking, they believe whatever they've *ever* been told. And some of us have woken up, and we're learning to question things. Small things. Big things. What is true and what is just a lie they told me to keep me asleep? And the more questions you ask the more questions you realize there are. And, you're right, it's not at all what you thought it would be. The world. Not just college. But the whole world.

ETHAN. Wait a minute. I do know your voice.

(He finally looks up.)

Enchilada!

SHELLEY. Oh my god, you know who I am?

*(A very **ANNOYED STUDENT** walks up to them.)*

ANNOYED STUDENT. *(Whispering.)* I know this is kind of cliché of me, but we're in a library so can you *shut the eff up*? Thanks so much.

*(Very **ANNOYED STUDENT** walks away.)*

(Whispering until indicated:)

ETHAN. I know who you are.

SHELLEY. You do? And you think I'm crazy, right?

ETHAN. No. Not crazy. A little. Yeah. I watched all of your videos when I was... I had to miss the first semester and...anyway, I had a lot of time and so I watched all of your...

SHELLEY. What's your name?

ETHAN. Ethan.

SHELLEY. Well, Ethan, it's so nice to meet a fan.

ETHAN. A fan? I guess.

SHELLEY. You watched them all. Are you a Flat Earther? I *never* meet Flat Earthers – no one in my family will talk to me anymore. I just live and breathe Flat Earth videos and...my research.

ETHAN. Oh, I'm not...no. I mean, I watched your videos, honestly, because my roommate is really into you...

SHELLEY. The roommate you tried to kiss?

ETHAN. Yeah. He got me hooked...

SHELLEY. Hooked.

(*Laughs.*)

I'm like heroine.

ETHAN. I'm not a Flat Earther, though.

SHELLEY. I think you must be open to new ideas because I asked if you thought I was crazy and you said *no* first. You ended on yes, but your instinct was *no*. There's a part of you, I think, that must be intrigued by what I believe, right?

ETHAN. About the earth being flat and all that?

SHELLEY. Yes.

ETHAN. Intrigued? Maybe. Hmm, but I think you're wrong. *Flat Earth?* Noooooo.

SHELLEY. But see, you let the thought in, and it's kinda worming around in your brain, isn't it? I don't think it will take long for you to start seeing the clues everywhere. Because they are *everywhere*.

ETHAN. I don't know, I kinda trust the scientists who have figured a lot of this stuff out...you know...it seems irration...

(*Suddenly,* **ETHAN** *sees the* **GUY** *who looks like his brother. He walks into the library.*)

Oh My God.

SHELLEY. What?

(*Silence as* **ETHAN** *stares. The* **GUY** *is rather otherworldly.*)

ETHAN. Do you see that guy?

SHELLEY. Yes. Is that your roommate who saved your life?

ETHAN. No, that's my brother.

SHELLEY. Oh, really?

ETHAN. I mean, he's not my brother. My brother died. A few months ago.

> (**SHELLEY** *is not sure what to say.*)

But there he is. That's him. He's following me.

SHELLEY. Your brother died?

ETHAN. Yes.

SHELLEY. But that's him right there?

ETHAN. I know it doesn't make...

SHELLEY. What was your brother's name?

ETHAN. Jeremy.

SHELLEY. *(Full voice.)* Jeremy!

ETHAN. Shhhh!

> (*The* **GUY** *who looks like Jeremy turns in response, then turns away. The very* **ANNOYED STUDENT** *walks by and makes a super annoyed face.*)

SHELLEY. He turned and looked when I said Jeremy. Maybe it is him. Maybe, maybe.

ETHAN. I think I'm going crazy.

SHELLEY. Maybe it is him. See what I mean, the clues are everywhere.

ETHAN. How does seeing a guy who looks like my dead brother mean that the earth is flat?

SHELLEY. I mean that there are more things that we don't understand than we care to admit. The Flat Earth was the beginning for me. Once I learned about *that* truth, the other mysteries started to become clearer and clearer to me. And now I see the world more for what it is, and I'm not, honestly, surprised that your brother could be here yet gone at the same time.

ETHAN. Okay, but...here's my big question about the Flat Earth.

SHELLEY. Yeah?

ETHAN. I mean, besides all the scientific facts that stand as really strong arguments against it...

SHELLEY. They don't – I can show you, there is so much evidence that we are being lied to. Who spreads these "facts"? Where did you learn them? Did you ever test them yourself, or did you just believe them?

ETHAN. Well. But my question is: What would be the purpose of a flat earth with a dome over it? If it's true, then someone had to have made it, and there would have to be a reason. I don't think there is a god, or, I don't think there's a god who, like, interacts with us but if the earth was flat and had this dome over it, we would be like some kind of experiment or terrarium, or ant farm, created by someone for his or her pleasure. Or for our protection. Or punishment. Or something. And what would that be, and why wouldn't we know?

SHELLEY. *(Talking full voice.)* Would you believe me, Ethan, if I told you that *that exact question* is why I am in the library today. Look at these books: *The God Mystery. Planet Earth: God's Terrarium? Is this Heaven or is this Hell?* Ethan, this is blowing my mind. You stumbled in here after nearly dying and you had all of these options for seats, and you sat down right next to *me*. You don't think that there's a god interacting with you today? The ghost of your dead brother was just in this room, as if he approved of our meeting, as if he led you to me.

ETHAN. That is pretty weird.

SHELLEY. You don't have to whisper, Ethan. Now that you're waking up, you can speak in a clear loud voice.

ANNOYED STUDENT. I will file an official complaint against you two, just so you know. I already called security.

SHELLEY. We don't care, do we Ethan? You have no power over us, because we are awake and you are asleep.

ANNOYED STUDENT. Oh, god, are you *high*? I'm so reporting you.

SHELLEY. Continue to bow to authority, you poor sleepwalking...

(*A* **SECOND ANNOYED STUDENT** *appears.*)

SECOND ANNOYED STUDENT. Can you guys keep all the noise down? Some of us are at this school to learn something.

ANNOYED STUDENT. They're high.

SHELLEY. We are high, aren't we Ethan?

ETHAN. Umm...

SHELLEY. Aren't we, Ethan?

ETHAN. Yeah.

SECOND ANNOYED STUDENT. I knew I should've gone to Xavier.

SHELLEY. No matter where you go, you will learn nothing.

ANNOYED STUDENT. The cops are literally on their way.

SHELLEY. Oh, LITERALLY? Come on Ethan, let's go. Let's go, *literally.*

Scene Seven
Detour Pt. 2

(**ETHAN** *and* **SHELLEY** *are with* **ANDRE**, *a charismatic, sincere man.*)

SHELLEY. Ayn Rand. Me, too! Ayn Rand. I was obsessed with Ayn Rand. Joined the Objectivist Society. That took away years of my life. Got over it. Then I became one of those know-it-all atheists. Got over it. I finally realized that identifying with a group was causing problems for me. I'm too easily persuadable and I just, boom, change my whole thing like *that.* I absolutely would have put on the Nikes and eaten the apple sauce.

(*They stare at her, unsure.*)

Heaven's Gate? Remember them? They castrated themselves and thought a spaceship was coming behind the Hale-Bopp comet? Phenobarbital, applesauce chaser?

ANDRE. Yes, of course.

SHELLEY. They actually thought there was an *outer space.* There are no comets, there are no spaceships! Hello! Not even *our* rockets make it into outer space, look it up! Look online! EVERY SINGLE rocket ship fades from sight but just as it's fading it kinda curves, like it's trying not to hit something up there, something *dome-like.* But, yeah, before I learned the truth about everything, I was a sucker for any bossy philosopher, Ayn Rand, Penn Jillette, any of those guys. They just argue *so well* and manage to seal up any little cracks that might let the doubt in. And before you know it, you're this little Ayn Rand zombie just spitting back cold little sentences of hers and you don't realize that she was secretly this emotional monster who just wanted complete control over her own bursting heart, not to mention complete control over all of humanity, her *subordinates.* What a cunt.

(*Silence.*)

(**ANDRE** *does not approve of that word.*)

Why am I saying this?

ANDRE. I'm not exactly sure, umm, Ethan was telling us that he's been having trouble *landing* here, that's the word you used, right? Landing. That these little winds keep pushing him – if you don't mind, Ethan, my imposing my own metaphors on your story!

ETHAN. No, no, it's fine.

ANDRE. These little winds keep...knocking him off-balance, or, no, no, I'm getting the image of the earth actually moving away from you as you are trying to find your footing.

ETHAN. Yeah, kind of. That's what it feels like.

ANDRE. So, go on.

SHELLEY. Well, she was *madly* in love with her disciple Nathaniel Branden, a man she couldn't have! So she *forced* him...

ANDRE. I meant Ethan go on.

SHELLEY. Oh. Yeah, go fuck yourself Ayn Rand. I'm *over you*! *Get out of my head!*

ETHAN. Umm...that's about it, really. I've come to college twice now and both times it's been disastrous on the first day of my arrival. I keep trying to move in...but... but...

ANDRE. Something won't let you.

ETHAN. Right.

ANDRE. Something is...*stopping* you.

ETHAN. Yeah, I can't seem to even get into my dorm room. I'm always...*stopped*, yeah...in the hallway. I can't get beyond the hallway.

ANDRE. Isn't that amazing?

ETHAN. What?

ANDRE. Just...the fact that...we all acknowledge that there is a force outside of ourselves that specifically influences us. That guides our...well, our very feet. We all feel that. Don't we? I do.

SHELLEY. I do.

ETHAN. I guess. Yeah.

ANDRE. Yeah. It's amazing. It's inherent in us *all*, this truth that we are not the ones in control. Even the way you said it in your story, you kept *trying* to move in, but *something* wouldn't let you. You had no real power.

SHELLEY. I just got goosebumps.

ETHAN. Wait, so, Andre, you think the earth is flat, too?

ANDRE. Umm...

SHELLEY. That's how we met. I left a comment on one of his YouTube videos and he reached out to me.

ETHAN. Oh?

ANDRE. I...have an online aspect of my ministry, yes, and I make videos that examine popular topics from a Christian perspective.

ETHAN. Your ministry? Like...

> *(Looks around.)*

...you mean your dorm room?

ANDRE. I think a ministry is not defined by the space so much as the spirit with which the space is filled. My ministry is humble, yes. Perhaps it's worth noting that the dorm room you've landed most successfully in is this one.

SHELLEY. *(To ETHAN.)* Isn't he amazing? I told you...

> *(To ANDRE.)* I told him he *had* to meet you.

> *(To ETHAN.)* He said that scholars have known that the earth is flat for thousands of years. It's in the Bible.

ANDRE. I made a video discussing the earth as the Bible paints it, yes...

SHELLEY. You believe that the earth is flat.

ANDRE. By virtue of the Bible, not by... I'm not a conspiracy guy. I believe the Bible. The Bible says the earth is flat, so it's never been a question for me.

SHELLEY. Isn't that wild?

ETHAN. The Bible says the earth is flat?

ANDRE. That's how many scholars read it, yes.

SHELLEY. It talks about the pillars, the firmament, the water above us, in the firmament, the dome, the creator, all of the things, essentially, that the flat-Earth movement has unearthed, so to speak.

ANDRE. I'm not a conspiracy theorist. I'm a Christian.

SHELLEY. I'm not a Christian, I'm a conspiracy theorist!

(She laughs, **ANDRE** *doesn't.)*

ANDRE. *Not a Christian?*

SHELLEY. No, no, I *am*, I *am*. I was just trying to be funny. It sounded funny, so I said it.

ANDRE. That's not...it's not *actually* funny to... I believe, deeply, that you are what you say you are. And you're not what you say you're not. Some people register their dogs as "service animals" so they can take them on planes and into restaurants. So they can skirt the rules, basically. Now, I'm not a rule-follower, I don't think we should blindly subject ourselves to every rule that our local governments impose, that's not my problem with people who register their dogs as "service animals" when they're not, my problem is, that I think it worms its way into one's soul, to say over and over, "I am a person who cannot function without the emotional support of my dog." Because that's what you're saying when you say your dog is an emotional support animal. And after a while, after you've said, "I am a person who cannot function without the emotional support of my dog" so many times, I believe that *you become a person who cannot function without the emotional support of your dog.*

(Silence.)

So saying something that is not true can in fact make it true.

(Silence.)

SHELLEY. I am a Christian. I wasn't always. I'm sorry.

(Silence.)

ANDRE. The hand of God is not meant to elude us. That's why we feel it so strongly. The danger is that we ignore it or deny it. He tells us in a million ways every day that he is with us and guiding us. And when we are doing what he is *not* guiding us to do, when we are sinning, we feel his disapproval as strongly. Don't we? I'm curious about what you told us earlier, Ethan. About your near-death experience.

ETHAN. *(Laughs a little.)* Choking on chips? It was embarrassing.

ANDRE. But hadn't your mouth – didn't you say? – hadn't your mouth led you to sin just moments before?

> *(**ETHAN** is silent.)*

Is it possible that whatever prevented you from *landing* in your dorm room is also what grabbed you by the throat at that moment?

> *(**ETHAN** is silent.)*

I think God is everywhere. And nothing is accidental. And unhappiness is not what he wants for us – are you happy, Ethan? Are you unhappy? What is God telling you?

> *(Silence. **ANDRE**'s thoughts are affecting **ETHAN**.)*

SHELLEY. 9/11. CERN. Vaccinations. Chemtrails. JFK. The moon. The Vietnam War. Death camps. Native Americans and smallpox. Salem. Catherine the Great. Rome. Cairo. Caesar. Pontius Pilate. Jesus. Moses. Cain and Abel. Eve. Adam.

> *(Silence.)*

God.

> *(Silence.)*

ETHAN. My brother died.

ANDRE. I'm sorry to hear that.

ETHAN. I feel so...so...yeah, it's just like you said...the earth spinning away from me, every time I try to step on it.

SHELLEY. It's not spinning. Is the thing. Think of it like a giant paper plate, rising.

ANDRE. *Shelley*.

ETHAN. I haven't... I don't know where my brother is. I don't know where *I* am. Do you remember? When you became you? Isn't it a little upsetting when you think about it – you just came into consciousness one day, one day all of the facts that are true about you started to present themselves. And there was nothing you could do to change any of it. This is who you are. This is where you live, this is when you live. This is your mother, and this is your father, and this is your sister, and this is your brother. And this is your heart and these are your feelings. And this is time. And this is hunger.

ANDRE. I know.

ETHAN. And then: where did my brother go? He was right here.

(*Silence.*)

ANDRE. I want to invite you to come on Sunday, because we're talking about that. I think you might find...that there are many other people with the same question.

Scene Eight
Crossroads

(In the same dorm hallway.)

*(**ETHAN** enters, wearing very plain clothes that somehow look wrong on him. It's like he's in costume for a character that he just isn't right for. The pants are pleated, khaki, the shirt does not fit well. It's too modest and ill-fitting.)*

(And his hair is different.)

(He walks to 802, puts his key in the lock, and opens the door.)

*(**DEREK** is inside.)*

DEREK. There you are! Ethan!

*(But **ETHAN** closes the door and walks quickly away.)*

*(**DEREK** opens the door, chasing after **ETHAN**.)*

Ethan! Ethan!

ETHAN. I'm sorry, I'll just come back when you're not there.

DEREK. What do you mean? ETHAN!

*(**ETHAN** stops.)*

What's going on with you? I've been looking for you, trying to call you, where have you been staying? I thought you'd left school again, are you okay? What are those clothes? Ethan, stop avoiding me, it doesn't matter, what happened. It's okay – I'm worried about you. Seriously, what are you wearing?

ETHAN. Clothes. Just clothes. Derek.

DEREK. Would you please just come into our room. Look: E is F. Ethan is Finally back. Please?

ETHAN. I can't.

DEREK. *Can't?*

ETHAN. I can't.

DEREK. Can't...? Can't...look, Ethan, you don't have to be embarrassed, it's all forgotten, it's not that big of a deal. I don't care. Honestly, you're making a tiny little thing into a silly, big deal. It was a *kiss*, it was a *kiss* that was actually...very sweet, come on, don't be this way.

ETHAN. It's not *that*. It's not that at all, that means nothing to me. I'm not, like, in love with you or whatever you're thinking. I'm not so tempted by you that I'm afraid to be alone with you. Because I'm not even...*any*way, so... I *can't...be...* A *kiss*, Derek, was the ultimate betrayal in history, remember, so let's not pretend that *a kiss* is impotent.

    (**DEREK** *is deeply confused.*)

Also, it's none of your business. I don't mean for that to sound...but it's...true. I'm gonna go. I'll just come back later.

DEREK. So, what, we're not friends anymore? Just like that?

ETHAN. It's not that simple.

DEREK. It's not?

ETHAN. I'm finally... I know who I...who I should...and it's not, it's not who I said I was and it's not who you think I am and it's not someone who kisses...that way... I don't want to explain. I don't have to explain myself to you. We're not. Like.

DEREK. What is it, Ethan, what's going on with you?

ETHAN. Nothing. *Everything. Everything.* Why do you care? We don't even know each other, really. And we're obviously...

DEREK. Okay. You don't have to explain yourself to me. I guess I thought we were going to be...like...friends. That first night, I got really excited, to make a friend. I really thought... I saw four years into the future, I swear. Our college time together. You know what they call that? In A.A.? I went to an A.A. meeting – can you believe that? I'm eighteen. A.A. Man. But they call it *reminiscing about the future.* I reminisced about our future friendship. In our future, we are roommates every year. Even off-campus. We become more and more different in big ways but somehow closer and better and better friends. To each other. And on graduation we are on this rooftop, some farewell party. But we don't say farewell because we know we'll be...like...best friends forever. And we're hugging and crying.

ETHAN. I need to surround myself with...people...like...who have the same...who are...

DEREK. Like, gay people? You want to be around more gay people?

ETHAN. I'm not gay.

DEREK. Yes you are.

ETHAN. I'm not. I don't think. I'm not... I have *feelings*...but it's not *who I am*. I think it's something I have to deal with, but I'm not going to let it...it's not... I'm...

DEREK. Are you okay? Should I be worried? You have the strangest...you...don't seem yourself.

ETHAN. *Myself?*

DEREK. Yeah.

(*Silence.* **ETHAN** *thinks about that.*)

ETHAN. What does E is F mean?

DEREK. Ethan is Finally here. You know that.

ETHAN. It doesn't mean that.

DEREK. If I say so.

ETHAN. Well, that's sloppy, it's not E is F H, like Ethan is Finally Here. It's E is F. What is E and what is F? And why is F really E? Why is E really F? It really annoys me!

DEREK. It means, I don't know, it means... I don't know. It was a tattoo I saw. A tattoo on this woman. Growing up. She was...you know there are people that just...are *the people* in your world, you see them but you don't know them, their names or anything, but they're constant. There's always that girl that works at that drugstore and that guy that walks his dog. I guess we are the people in *their* world, too. But this woman...she looked so...*dead*. She looked like she'd died, and learned the truth of the world. Like she was a ghost – I never talked about her to anyone, maybe nobody else saw her, maybe she *was* a ghost. Don't know anything about her. But she had this tattoo, right here, and I got close enough to her one day to see that it said *E is F*. She saw me seeing her tattoo and she said: *Ahh, figure that one out, and you know the secret.* She was probably just crazy, probably, but... I kinda want to figure it out. E is F. Everyone is Fake. Empathy is Fleeting. Extremism is Flawed. I don't know.

> *(Long pause.)*

ETHAN. Well. I'm gonna go.

DEREK. If you tell me right now that you need me, or you need my help in some way, I will help you. Do you need my help right now? Is someone...?

> *(Silence.)*

Okay. Ethan. I don't know why this is so sad. You're not leaving school, right?

ETHAN. No.

DEREK. You're just...

ETHAN. Yeah. I'm just.

> *(**ETHAN** starts to go.)*

DEREK. For the record, even though it's none of my business: I feel like this isn't you.

ETHAN. Noted.

> *(**ETHAN** walks to the elevator.)*

Scene Nine
Going Up

(**ETHAN** *steps onto the elevator.*)

(*He is not alone.*)

(*The* **GUY** *who looks like his brother is on the elevator as well.*)

(**ETHAN** *looks at* **GUY WHO LOOKS LIKE JEREMY**.)

GUY WHO LOOKS LIKE JEREMY. Hello.

ETHAN. (*Silence.*) What's your name?

GUY WHO LOOKS LIKE JEREMY. Jeremy.

(**ETHAN** *laughs nervously.*)

What's *your* name?

ETHAN. You don't know?

GUY WHO LOOKS LIKE JEREMY. No. Should I? Do I know you?

ETHAN. Ethan.

GUY WHO LOOKS LIKE JEREMY. Hello, Ethan.

ETHAN. (*Nervous laugh.*) Jeremy?

GUY WHO LOOKS LIKE JEREMY. Yeah?

ETHAN. All the way up?

GUY WHO LOOKS LIKE JEREMY. Sorry?

ETHAN. Are you going to the roof...for the...

GUY WHO LOOKS LIKE JEREMY. Oh, yup. Yup.

(**ETHAN** *is silent.*)

I've seen you, on the campus.

(*Silence.*)

Around.

(*Silence.*)

There are some people who just *people* your world, you know, like extras walking around that you see all the time but you know nothing about?

ETHAN. Yeah.

GUY WHO LOOKS LIKE JEREMY. Have I been that for you? Too?

ETHAN. Well. In a way. In a way. You look...so...familiar.

GUY WHO LOOKS LIKE JEREMY. You, too. You, too.

(*Silence.*)

One could measure their entire college experience in elevator rides, couldn't they? Four years pass pretty quickly just going up and down, up and down doors opening on a day, closing on a day. Time.

ETHAN. I guess.

GUY WHO LOOKS LIKE JEREMY. Hmm.

ETHAN. Hmm.

GUY WHO LOOKS LIKE JEREMY. What happens?

ETHAN. Sorry?

GUY WHO LOOKS LIKE JEREMY. In your first year of college?

ETHAN. I'm not sure what you mean.

GUY WHO LOOKS LIKE JEREMY. I think you do.

ETHAN. (*Looks at him strangely, then.*) I...it's actually something I'm a little ashamed of. I...pick a time when I know that Derek, my roommate isn't going to be in our room, and I move all of my stuff out and into a different dorm altogether. I never even say goodbye to him.

GUY WHO LOOKS LIKE JEREMY. Why not?

ETHAN. Chicken. I guess I know that I'm doing something cowardly and so I'm embarrassed about it. Can't look him in the eye or talk about it. But it's not wrong at the time, honestly, I mean, it seems like the *right* thing, I'm just all mixed-up because... I made these new friends, religious friends, and...it's persuasive, what they're saying to me. I am persuaded. Which happens to me a lot! If you think about it. Oh my god. I get persuaded into being someone I'm not...like...all the time. A guy with purple hair, or the father in my mother's house, or...straight. Or, like in high school, I read Ayn Rand and suddenly I became this complete asshole.

GUY WHO LOOKS LIKE JEREMY. I think that happens to a lot of people.

ETHAN. I met a girl – same thing happened to her.

GUY WHO LOOKS LIKE JEREMY. We're not alone. Even in our errors.

ETHAN. It takes me a while to shake free from it. So, to answer your question, in my first year...

> *(Laughs.)*

It's ridiculous. I become a born-again Christian. *What am I doing?*

> (**ANDRE** *gets on the elevator.*)

ANDRE. The end of freshman year you stop coming to church. I call you to check in and you have an excuse always for not coming. God is not interested in excuses, I say to you, but I know I'm losing you. It's okay. We lose our sheep. They wander into the woods and some of them find their way back to us, some of them get eaten by wolves. I can't be responsible, at a certain point. Ethan. Ethan. Come back to us. Ethan. I know it's hard and I know there are temptations, I know how seductive the world can be, but it's all an illusion and one day it will flicker out, like a cheap party lightbulb, and you will be in the dark. But I know the way to the light. You just have to follow me. If you don't follow me right now I'll assume you have no interest in your own salvation.

> (**ANDRE** *gets off the elevator.*)

GUY WHO LOOKS LIKE JEREMY. Is that hard?

ETHAN. Yeah. One day, I said to Andre in this casual way something about, "Well, we're all just marching toward our graves," trying to say that there's no one better way to live than any other, and he burst into tears and said he was so sorry for me, that because of that one sentence, I was going to burn, physically, literally, burn, my skin, my hair, my eyes, in fire, for all eternity. He cried, cried, because I think he genuinely cares. About people, about me, he's a good guy, I think, but I stopped going to church after that. That was the end of freshman year.

GUY WHO LOOKS LIKE JEREMY. And a year passed just like that?

ETHAN. *(Laughs.)* Yeah. So fast!

GUY WHO LOOKS LIKE JEREMY. What about year two? What happens.

ETHAN. I move off-campus. My sister comes to visit me. And stays for a while.

  *(**JENNIFER** gets on the elevator.)*

JENNIFER. I'm not speaking to Mom ever again. She told me, she actually said this, that Jeremy had such promise in life and *isn't it ironic that the child who has no ambition is the one who lives*. She *said* that. Just frosting fucking Christmas tree cookies. I mean, I *was* still working at the Lube and Dash – I finally get why that's so funny to you, by the way – and had officially dropped out of high school, so she wasn't wrong that my ambition was...stalled, but for crap's sake! So can I live with you? Cincinnati is better than Denver because it's *almost* by the ocean which is *almost* Europe. I heard a joke about London, which I don't get, but it's made me want to move to London. Here it is: What's the best thing about London? *Paris*. I guess it's really funny if you get it but I think I won't get it unless I move to London. I was thinking about San Francisco, but the joke I heard about San Francisco made me reconsider. San Francisco: a million people, a thousand stories. So can I stay with you and I'll just save money and then move to London?

  *(**JENNIFER** exits the elevator.)*

GUY WHO LOOKS LIKE JEREMY. She's hilarious.

ETHAN. I know.

GUY WHO LOOKS LIKE JEREMY. Who's Jeremy?

ETHAN. Our brother. He died.

GUY WHO LOOKS LIKE JEREMY. My name is Jeremy.

ETHAN. I know.

GUY WHO LOOKS LIKE JEREMY. Does she stay with you?

ETHAN. Yes, for the entire year. It's actually nice. She makes good on her promise and doesn't speak to my mom and does move to London. She's still there. Not speaking to my mom and I don't know what she does there, exactly, but she seems to like it. I wish I were as brave as she is.

GUY WHO LOOKS LIKE JEREMY. And a year passes just like that.

ETHAN. Yes.

> (**DEREK** *gets on the elevator.*)
>
> (*Awkward silence.*)
>
> (*Long, horrible awkward silence.*)
>
> (**DEREK** *gets off the elevator.*)

GUY WHO LOOKS LIKE JEREMY. What was that about?

ETHAN. That's Derek. That's what we do when we see each other for our entire sophomore year.

GUY WHO LOOKS LIKE JEREMY. No words.

ETHAN. He's very upset with me and I'm too embarrassed to apologize.

GUY WHO LOOKS LIKE JEREMY. A whole year passes like that?

ETHAN. Yup.

GUY WHO LOOKS LIKE JEREMY. That's a long time. And a short time.

> (*A young man,* **KEVIN**, *gets on the elevator.*)

KEVIN. I'll pick you up on Wednesday and we'll drive up to my place and have a quiet holiday together. Won't that be nice?

ETHAN. Okay, wonderful.

GUY WHO LOOKS LIKE JEREMY. You like him?

ETHAN. He's the guy I start dating in my junior year.

GUY WHO LOOKS LIKE JEREMY. You have a *boyfriend*?

ETHAN. Well. It doesn't...

GUY WHO LOOKS LIKE JEREMY. Fellow student?

ETHAN. No. No. He lives in a small town about an hour away. We meet at a bar downtown.

KEVIN. I tell you my name in the bar, but it's so loud. I yell, "It's KEVIN!" And then the rest of the night you keep calling me Peter, and I'm too embarrassed to correct you.

ETHAN. I think he's a better Peter than a Kevin, don't you?

GUY WHO LOOKS LIKE JEREMY. Is he your first boyfriend?

ETHAN. Kinda. Yeah. Yeah. Late bloomer.

KEVIN. I will be right back.

> (**KEVIN** *exits the elevator.*)
>
> (*Silence.*)

ETHAN. He's not coming back.

GUY WHO LOOKS LIKE JEREMY. No?

ETHAN. (*Laughs.*) It's stupid. It's too sad and too...

GUY WHO LOOKS LIKE JEREMY. What happens?

ETHAN. (*Sigh.*) He...okay. It's melodramatic and obnoxious, do you want to hear it?

GUY WHO LOOKS LIKE JEREMY. Of course I do, now!

ETHAN. My mom...since my brother...

GUY WHO LOOKS LIKE JEREMY. Died.

ETHAN. Right.

GUY WHO LOOKS LIKE JEREMY. How *is* Mom?

ETHAN. What?

GUY WHO LOOKS LIKE JEREMY. How is your mom?

ETHAN. Well, she...she's always been a person who looks like she's about to fall into a swimming pool. You know? Always bracing and never...firm. So when Jeremy... it's like she finally fell in. And there were pills to help her out, but then the pills swallowed her up. So – this year...

GUY WHO LOOKS LIKE JEREMY. Your third year. Already!

ETHAN. I know! I'm supposed to go home for Thanksgiving
because my mom is very sad, all of her children are
gone – my dad left years ago...tragic, right? Horrible.
Jennifer's not speaking to her. All that. I tell her I'll
come home. And then...I'm out at a bar one night and
I meet...

GUY WHO LOOKS LIKE JEREMY. Kevin.

ETHAN. Peter.

GUY WHO LOOKS LIKE JEREMY. Ha.

ETHAN. And we start hanging out and suddenly I'm in
love and we listen to Kate Bush albums all night and...
I'm so...happy. And he says, *What are you doing for
Thanksgiving?* And I say, *Going home.* And he says,
Too bad. And I say, *Why too bad?* And he says, *Well,
I have no plans and I thought you and I could make
Thanksgiving dinner together, just the two of us.* And
I have never been lovesick, so I don't recognize the
symptoms. My heart is in my throat, I say, yes, yes, let's
have Thanksgiving at your house. I call my mom to tell
her that, well, that she'll have to spend Thanksgiving
without me – which means alone – because I've got
to stay in Cincinnati for some urgent school-related
something. She knows I'm lying. But says okay. And
I hang up. And the morning arrives when Peter is
picking me up. And he's late. And then he's really late.
So I call, no answer. And then he's hours late, and I call
and no answer. And then it's the evening and he's not
there and it's midnight and he's not there, and it's the
next day, Thanksgiving Day, and he's not there and I'm
still kinda sitting by the door with my little bag packed
waiting.

GUY WHO LOOKS LIKE JEREMY. That's so sad.

ETHAN. *(Laughs.)* It's so stupid! Thanksgiving after like
three dates?

GUY WHO LOOKS LIKE JEREMY. Does he ever show up?

ETHAN. No. And he never answers the phone. And he never
calls. And I never, absolutely never hear from him

again. Of course, he just didn't know how to end it, so he "ghosted" me, that's what it's called. When you just... disappear on someone.

GUY WHO LOOKS LIKE JEREMY. Ghost.

ETHAN. Yeah. Sometimes I think, *Maybe he actually died. Maybe he died and I'll never know.*

GUY WHO LOOKS LIKE JEREMY. He didn't die.

ETHAN. I know.

GUY WHO LOOKS LIKE JEREMY. Do you have a boyfriend now?

ETHAN. No, not really. Dating. Lotta bozos out there.

GUY WHO LOOKS LIKE JEREMY. Funny. And a year passes like that? Dating?

ETHAN. Yup. Yup.

>*(**DEREK** gets on the elevator again.)*
>
>*(Awkward silence.)*

DEREK. *(Awkward.)* Hey, Ethan.

ETHAN. *(Awkward.)* Hi, Derek.

DEREK. How are you? How's...?

ETHAN. Good. Good. You?

DEREK. Pretty good.

>*(Silence.)*

I wrecked my car. That was a bad. Moment.

ETHAN. Were you drinking?

DEREK. No. I told you I quit. When I quit I quit.

ETHAN. Sorry.

DEREK. It's actually a funny story.

>*(Silence as **DEREK** waits for **ETHAN** to engage.)*

ETHAN. Oh?

DEREK. You know when it snowed really bad in February – and the streets were all ice?

ETHAN. Yeah.

DEREK. I turned down McMillan and my brakes just... wouldn't stop me from sliding right down the hill. Just

– ice. There was no one on the road, thankfully because I couldn't stop – I'm sliding right down the hill toward this house. And I'm going, *No no no no no no no no,* but wham! I slam right into their front steps. Concrete. Thankfully. No damage to the house, smashed up my car. Well, right next door was my friend's house – this is the funny part – and so I kinda staggered over there, dazed, and let myself in, he was in his room taking a nap. I said, "John – I wrecked my car, right next door," and he didn't get out of bed or anything he just said, "Oh, really? Are you okay?" and I said, "Yeah, I think so... I think so..." and he never got out of bed or even got up to see the wreck and it was awkward so I...left. Thinking, *What a bad friend. He didn't even get out of bed.* And then a few days later I'm walking on campus and he comes running up to me and says, "Dude, I'm so sorry. Are you okay? When you came over and told me you wrecked your car I was in bed jerking off and I didn't want to get up and hug you."

> (**ETHAN** *laughs.*)

> (**GUY WHO LOOKS LIKE JEREMY** *laughs.*)

> (**DEREK** *laughs.*)

ETHAN. *(Not sexual, just true.)* I would have.

DEREK. Yeah, man. I know. I know. I'll see you later.

> (**DEREK** *exits the elevator.*)

GUY WHO LOOKS LIKE JEREMY. And so you're friends. Again?

ETHAN. We're talking again.

GUY WHO LOOKS LIKE JEREMY. And a whole year passes like that?

ETHAN. Yeah. Talking.

GUY WHO LOOKS LIKE JEREMY. And so.

ETHAN. Yeah. My senior year.

> (**SHELLEY** *gets on the elevator.*)

SHELLEY. Ethan! Hi!

ETHAN. Hi, Shelley! Long time.

SHELLEY. I know, I know Are you...

    (She points up.)

...?

ETHAN. Yup.

SHELLEY. I will be so relieved to get the hell out of ACADEMIA! The mind-control of it all. Why am I still here? I've been spying on the enemy for LONG ENOUGH now. I'm ready to take everything I've learned and Un-Learn it.

ETHAN. Are you still doing your flat-earth show?

SHELLEY. *(Disappointed.)* Awww. You don't watch anymore?

ETHAN. Umm... *(Sheepish.)*

SHELLEY. It's okay. It's okay. It's gonna take a while. To make everyone see. The truth. The truth is...you know what *the truth* is? The *truth* is horrible. That's why everyone ignores it. Because the *truth* is belittling. It towers over you and you can't fight it. So, it's okay that you turned away from the truth. It's not fun to look at. I sat on a jury once, horrible trial, lasted five weeks, about these waitresses at a hotel who had been sexually harassed and psychologically blackmailed by their supervisor. Anyway, there was one waitress who told a devastating story on the witness stand about a specific day, at a specific time, when specific horrible things happened at the hands of her abuser. She told us about the agonizing *full one hour* that the supervisor kept her trapped in a room and took advantage of her. I was weeping. As a juror you can. Weep. You can also eat candy, they don't care, as you're breathing and awake. But *THAT* is another story, the American Legal System. Huh! Sham! Lies! Hypocrisy! Anyway. She finishes this awful story and the defense attorney for the toadish little man who was her abuser stood up and wheeled in a television screen with a computer attached to it and played a video from a security camera for us with a date and time-stamp in the corner. He said, *Is this the date in question?* She said

Yes. Is this the time in question? She said, *Yes. Is this you and the defendant walking down the hall, entering this room.* She shuddered as she said, *Yes.* She looked at me, directly at me, in the eye, with this look that said, "Now you'll see just what I'm talking about. This was the worst day of my life." And so the lawyer played the clip. And the waitress and the supervisor disappeared behind this door, and the little timestamp in the corner of this security footage ticked through the seconds and I thought, *Oh, no, we're going to have to watch an entire hour tick past, because that's how long she was in there with him.* But before I finished that thought, the door in the security video opened, and she and the supervisor exited the room calmly. And we all gasped. Including the waitress. Because an hour *had not* passed, but only fifteen seconds. And she was looking around as if God himself had walked in and called her a liar. But we knew *she wasn't lying*, or at least I did, but *the truth* was wagging its finger right in her face. She sobbed. Because she *wasn't lying*. She was not lying. Only, the truth was not what she remembered. Exactly. It was horrible. She crumbled under the weight of the truth. So I understand not liking the truth. But I, personally, just cannot hide from it anymore. Wherever it leads, I'm embracing the truth, it's beyond the Flat Earth now, it's the WHOLE ENCHILADA! The whole terrible enchilada.

(The elevator doors open.)

Oh, well, here we are. Con-*grad*-ulations, as they say. I burned my diploma as soon as they handed it to me.

*(She shows **ETHAN** her lighter.)*

I screamed: I didn't even want your Master's Degree!

(Laughs.)

What is *wrong* with me?

(She exits, shouting:)

Burn Your Diploma! Burn Your Diploma!

GUY WHO LOOKS LIKE JEREMY. I like her. Flat Earth?

ETHAN. Me, too. Yeah, I know.

(Getting off the elevator.)

Are you coming? It's a nice little rooftop graduation party.

GUY WHO LOOKS LIKE JEREMY. Oh, no. I'm going back.

ETHAN. Okay.

(Sudden sadness.)

GUY WHO LOOKS LIKE JEREMY. Happy graduation. Congrats.

ETHAN. Bye, Jeremy. I'm glad we finally talked. I've been seeing you for so...

GUY WHO LOOKS LIKE JEREMY. Me, too. Me, too.

ETHAN. Okay, well.

GUY WHO LOOKS LIKE JEREMY. Okay.

ETHAN. Oh, I forgot to say that throughout all of the years here, you were...always...

GUY WHO LOOKS LIKE JEREMY. You, too. It was nice to meet you.

ETHAN. Yeah.

GUY WHO LOOKS LIKE JEREMY. See ya.

ETHAN. Bye, Jeremy. Bye.

(Elevator doors close.)

Scene Ten
Taking Off

(A rooftop graduation party.)

(All are assembled, some in robes and caps. Eating cake.)

*(**DEREK** is there. After some awkward milling, **ETHAN** approaches him.)*

ETHAN. Well.

DEREK. Yep.

ETHAN. Yep.

DEREK. You all right?

ETHAN. I...woke up in the middle of the night, maybe this was...like...two years ago...and I realized: Oh, god, I never even said Thank You to Derek when he saved my life.

DEREK. Saved your life?

ETHAN. The Heimlich maneuver?

DEREK. *(Laughs.)* Oh, man! Right.

ETHAN. You saved my life.

DEREK. You were choking!

ETHAN. And you saved me. I would be... I would be *dead* without you. Dead.

DEREK. No. No. Come on.

ETHAN. Listen: Thank you for saving my life.

DEREK. Okay. You're welcome. It did feel pretty good. I'm a hero.

> *(They both laugh.)*

Didn't you think we would be better friends?

ETHAN. Yeah.

DEREK. I saved your life but I lost you even so.

ETHAN. See, it's 'cause you say things like *that*.

DEREK. What?

ETHAN. Nothing.

DEREK. Man. That flew by, huh?

ETHAN. Yes. Yes.

DEREK. Where you going?

ETHAN. New York.

DEREK. Yuck. Chicago.

ETHAN. Yuck.

> *(They laugh.)*

I can't shake the feeling that...there is a gap between us...that I want to close, what is it? I am embarrassed, by how I behaved, by ghosting you the way I did, and I feel like I *owe* you my life, my entire life, how can I repay that? I am at a deficit, with you. A gratitude deficit.

DEREK. Maybe if you ever had to save my life, that would erase the deficit?

ETHAN. Maybe.

DEREK. Come here.

> *(**DEREK** walks to the edge of the rooftop. Gets very near the edge.)*

ETHAN. What are you doing?

DEREK. Come here. Come closer.

> *(**ETHAN** moves closer.)*

ETHAN. Derek! You are so close to the edge, please, please, it's making me...

DEREK. I'm going to lean away from you, and if you don't grab me, I'm going to fall. Okay?

ETHAN. Derek! You can't be serious.

DEREK. Don't make a scene about this, it's just between us. You're going to save my life right now.

ETHAN. Derek.

DEREK. You're going to save my life. And then we'll be even. And then for our entire lives, we will be friends who saved each other's lives. And I can see the future, I think: we stay in touch, sometimes we're close, sometimes years pass and we don't speak, because we're busy with our lives, but nothing can take away the fact that we are each only here because the other saved our life. Isn't that kind of beautiful? It's not creepy, right? Ready?

ETHAN. Derek, oh, god.

DEREK. Just do it. I'm leaning away in three seconds. You have to save my life.

ETHAN. Derek.

DEREK. One...

ETHAN. Shit.

DEREK. Two...

ETHAN. You're a fucking poet.

DEREK. Three...

> (**DEREK** *leans away and* **ETHAN** *grabs him and pulls him to safety.*)
>
> (*They stand, hugging each other on the rooftop, laughing or crying or both. It's a quiet moment between two young men who will be friends forever.*)
>
> (*Lights fade.*)

The End